**Every Night at HOBO is Like a Great Party**

They start arriving about twelve-thirty or one o'clock. Golden-haired girls in cowboy outfits, backless tops, see-through dresses. The wilder the better. And elegant debs, the older society group. The rich Greeks and Arabs. The rock stars and latest young actors. Anybody famous who's in town. Young writers, designers, photographers, models.

And everybody wants to know me, Tony Blake. You wouldn't believe, the ladies practically fight to climb in the sack with me. You would think I was doing them a favor, and listen the way things have been going, I think I am.

It's a great life if you don't weaken. . . .

**THE STUD**

# Jackie Collins

A SIGNET BOOK
NEW AMERICAN LIBRARY

PUBLISHER'S NOTE

This novel is a work of fiction. Names, characters, places, and incidents either are the product of the author's imagination or are used fictitiously, and any resemblance to actual persons, living or dead, events, or locales is entirely coincidental.



Published by arrangement with the author.

SIGNET TRADEMARK REG. U.S. PAT. OFF. AND FOREIGN COUNTRIES
REGISTERED TRADEMARK—MARCA REGISTRADA
HECHO EN CHICAGO, U.S.A.

SIGNET, SIGNET CLASSIC, MENTOR, PLUME, MERIDIAN AND NAL BOOKS are published by New American Library, 1633 Broadway, New York, New York 10019

First Signet Printing, June, 1971

18 19 20 21

PRINTED IN THE UNITED STATES OF AMERICA

# THE STUD

# 1

# TONY

## LONDON 1969

There is something very exciting about the beginning of the evening—well the beginning of my evening, which is usually about ten-thirty, eleven o'clock. Every night at Hobo is like a party—a great party where everyone knows and likes everyone else.

They start coming in slowly. First the ones that want to be sure of a good table, then the watchers. Usually this whole group is stacked neatly out of the way on the wrong side of the room or, if they are really rough, in the back room. We've got a closed membership, but a few managed to find their way in. Then everyone sits around waiting for the swingers, and about twelve-thirty, one o'clock they start arriving. Golden-haired girls in cowboy outfits, Indian gear, boots, backless topless see-through dresses. The wilder the better. Their escorts varying from the long-haired mob of rock groups to the latest young actors. Elegant young debs in full evening dress, with chinless wonder escorts. The older society group. The rich Greeks. The even richer Arabs. An odd movie star. An odd M.P. or visiting senator. Anybody famous who's in town. Young writers, dress designers, photographers, models. They all come to look and be looked at, to see their friends. It's like a building excitement—reaching a breathless climax at around two A.M. when the room is so jammed you couldn't get anyone else in except maybe Frank Sinatra or Mick Jagger.

It seems ridiculous that six months ago they would hand me a pound or two and wouldn't recognize me if we passed in the street. Now they couldn't wait to grab hold of me. "Dahling" —kiss-kiss-kiss—"Who's here tonight?" Sly grab if the boy friend or husband wasn't looking. "Please don't give us a lousy table like last time"—affectionate squeeze and promising look. Then husband or boy friend steps forward—firm handshake, a few masculine chummy words, and I hand them over to Franco, swinging head-waiter supreme, who whisks them off to whatever table their position rates: the watchers on one side of the room, the doers on the other. All very neat, the duds with the bread tucked firmly away in the back room.

Yeah, I'm very popular now, everyone wants to know me. Funny thing isn't it? I'm the same guy, talk in the same voice, the clothes are a little more expensive, but that's about the only difference. You wouldn't believe it though, the ladies practically fight to climb in the sack with me. You would think I was doing them a big favor, and listen, the way things have been going I think I am!

I tell you it's a great life if you don't weaken.

Well, I suppose you're wondering how this all came about, how a guy like me, Tony Schwartzburg from somewhere near the Elephant and Castle, turned into Tony Blake, man about town, friend of the stars, host at the most "in" discotheque, Hobo. I have exchanged confidences such as "Where can we get some pot?" and "Got any birds?" with some of the most famous in the land. "Tony can arrange anything" is a well-known catch phrase around town.

Well, to begin with, I had the same useless tough life as most of the kids in my neighborhood—fighting in the back streets, watching in on the fights at home. My parents, Sadie and Sam, were a nice old Jewish couple who hated each other. Sam couldn't care less about me, but to Sadie the sun shone out of my left ear.

"Learn a trade, like your cousin Leon," she would say; "let the family be proud of you." I got laid at thirteen, just before I got barmitzvahed. If the family had known they'd have been proud of me! The girl—she was a few years older than me—gave me the crabs, and I spent about six months alternately trying to get rid of them and passing them on to any girl who got lucky! Eventually I passed them on to the wrong girl, and everyone found out. Sadie had hysterics and Sam patted me on the back and bought me some ointment.

By the time I was sixteen, I had been through a variety of jobs. Delivering papers, sweeping up in a factory, ushering at the local cinema—I got fired from that when the manager found me making it with a bird in the back row of the stalls. She was his best usherette and he was screwing her at the same time so he was a bit choked up. Unfortunately I knocked her up, and there was a family scandal, but seeing the manager wanted her back, as good usherettes were hard to come by, he paid for her abortion and everything was all right.

By this time Sadie and Sam were getting a bit fed up with me, and who can blame them? Sam stopped screaming at Sadie and started in on me. It was a good job someone thought of Uncle Bernie.

Uncle Bernie was the success of the family.

He owned two delicatessens and had sort of cut himself off from the rest of his clan. Anyway Sadie felt that as she was his only sister he owed her a favor, and she dragged me down to his place in Great Portland Street and insisted he give me a job. He wasn't too thrilled at the prospect, but knowing he wasn't going to get rid of Sadie any other way, he agreed.

He had a daughter, Marion, a big strapping girl with lots of thick black hair—everywhere. You name a place, Marion had thick black hair there. She wasn't bad apart from that, a bit sexy looking. Big tits and a thin, crooked nose. I suppose I shouldn't have, I mean she was my cousin and all, but one day the opportunity arose, and if the opportunity arises, who am I to put it down? Of course Uncle Bernie found out and there ended my career in the delicatessen business. It was all too much for Sadie, and even Sam wasn't too pleased.

Life at the Elephant was becoming a drag anyway, and having got as far as Great Portland Street, I thought why not go a bit further. I got a job as a dishwasher at the Savoy, and a room in Camden Town. Life was great. I entered my twenties a happy man.

I met a girl, Evie, a pretty curly-haired blonde. She was a hostess at a clip joint. She fixed me up with a job as a waiter, and I discovered the world of tips. It was great, taught me a lot about people. Taught me the right way to milk a pound from a drunk whose intention was to leave nothing.

I was making twenty quid a week. I branched out to striped Italian suits and pointed shoes, then dated girls with a bit more class, hair-dressers, shop assistants, and all that group. Not bad. I felt like a king! Visited the Elephant on Sundays, and handed Sadie a fiver. Of course she never took it, she always came out with a speech about how I should save my money, settle down, look for a nice Jewish girl and get married, be like cousin Leon—in my book a real schmuck.

I left the clip joint and started as a busboy in a high-class restaurant, not so much bread but a road to better things. And the better things were all around me. The birds that came into that place. Beautiful! Furs, jewelry, expensive smells.

From there I started as a waiter in another high-class place where I became involved with Penny, daughter of the owner. Penny was something else. She had red hair, was very neat, small and compact. I suppose I fell in love with her. Couldn't make it, that was probably why. Looking back on it now I reckon she was undersexed, but at the time it bothered me a lot. She was the first girl that I had wanted and couldn't have.

I don't want to sound conceited, but imagine a taller Tony Curtis with a touch of Michael Caine and Kris Kristofferson!

Anyway Penny and I wanted to get married. Her father of course was furious, but she got around him and, since he didn't want his daughter marrying a waiter, he opened a new place and put me in charge—as a sort of a deluxe headwaiter.

It all started there. That's where I first saw Fontaine.

Of course everyone's heard of Fontaine Khaled, she's sort of like a national institution, though not so old—around thirty-five I'd say, but even now I still don't know the truth.

Fontaine looks very haughty upper-class English. Beautiful of course, with chiseled bones (whether by nature or cosmetic surgery no one knows), a fine parchment skin, and angular bony body which lends itself to fancy clothes and long dark hair pulled back.

When I first saw her I couldn't take my eyes off. Here was a lady. Sounds corny I know, but there was no mistaking the fact. She had been a world-famous photographic model, and had retired to marry Benjamin Al Khaled, billionaire. She was always in the papers, jetting here, there, everywhere. Showing us around her villa in Acapulco, her castle in Spain, her town house in London or penthouse in New York.

I read the columns a lot; in my business it's always good to know who's who. So as soon as she came in I knew who she was. She was with three men and two women all of the same social scene, but not in the same class as her. I led them to their table personally, a thing I had stopped doing when I took over the place. I even referred to her by name just to let her know I was around. But she didn't give me a glance. So much for the instant impact of Tony Blake.

There was no husband with her, and I didn't think she was anyone's date. They were very square, the fellows with her, typical no-balls types, with loud public-school voices.

She was wearing what I thought was a rabbit coat, but later—during an intensive course in social education—I discovered that it was chinchilla. I thought I was pretty hip then, but I didn't even know a Gucci handbag from a Marks & Sparks.

I hovered around the table a lot, but not so much as a look.

I eavesdropped—"St. Moritz is becoming a terrible bore." "Did you know Jamie broke his leg in Tibet?" "Do you *believe* St. Laurent this year?' Pretty dull snatches of conversation.

The guy that paid the bill left a nothing tip.

Two nights later she was back, this time with her husband. He was much older than she.

They were with another old guy. She threw me a brief smile on her way in, which startled me, and after that they came in a lot, whenever they weren't flying around the world.

Penny was causing me problems. Since her father had promoted me, so to speak, I was having a fair amount of success. Customers liked me, I remembered their names, I saw their food was just right, and I became casually friendly with some of them. The place developed a good reputation, and people were disappointed if I wasn't there. They liked to be greeted by name and made to feel important.

Penny's father realized I was good for the joint, and I realized Penny was no good for me. It was not a good situation. She started to get very narky and jealous, accusing me of all sorts of things, most of which were true. Well I don't know if she thought I was jerking off or what, but I certainly wasn't getting any action from her. I moved to a small one-room flat off the Edgware Road and she caught me there one day with a red-haired croupier—female of course! What tears and scenes! She even offered me her virginity, but by that time I didn't even want it. So we parted bad friends.

Needless to say it was just a matter of time before her father and I would also part company. I had my eyes open for another job. By that time I had had the waiter bit, I wanted to move up in the world, progress. The ideal situation would be to get my own little place, but for that I needed bread.

I cast my eyes around and one memorable night they met squarely with Fontaine's. It was one of those looks, her cool aquamarine eyes clashed straight on with my moody dark stare (many's the bird who's told me I've got a moody dark stare) and that was it. We both knew something had to give.

She went to the ladies room shortly after and I was waiting when she came out.

"Tony," she said—she had a deep, very English, clipped accent—"you're wasting yourself here. Why don't you drop by and see me tomorrow? I have an idea that maybe you can help me with." She handed me a small hand-engraved card with her address, and added, "About three o'clock will be fine."

I nodded dumbly. To tell you the truth, I was knocked out by the whole thing.

I must have changed my outfit ten times the next day—was a casual look best or should I go for the slightly formal Italian gear? I finally settled for a pale lilac shirt with a stiff white collar, and a black silk suit.

I arrived a half-hour early at this knockout pad she had in Belgravia. It was too much! I found out it was an ex-embassy. They even had a swimming pool.

A butler settled me down in what I supposed was the living room, but it turned out to be just a waiting room. It was all expensive, with crazy carved furniture, and jazzy old pictures on the wall. Some of them were a bit naughty—there was one with three birds and one guy, but just when I was studying it closer, Fontaine came in. "Are you interested in art, Tony?" she asked. She looked great in a long sort of silk robe and her hair all loose.

Man, I can still remember how nervous I was. This was real class.

"Let's go into the study," she said. "Would you care for a drink?"

I asked for a sherry, figuring it was the thing to have.

"You don't look like a sherry man to me," she said, her eyes cool and amused.

I started to get excited there and then, and in the tight black trousers I was wearing that was no joke. I approached her warily; she didn't back away. In fact she came toward me. I put my arms around her. She was tall, and I could feel her bones through the thin robe. She fastened her arms about my neck and pulled my mouth onto hers. It was some kiss. She was like a hungry animal pushing and probing with her tongue, biting and sighing. I think I can safely say I gave back as good as I got.

"Let's go upstairs," she said at last, and added, "it's all right, Benjamin is away."

I followed her to a small elevator and we pressed closely together as it started up. She unzipped my trousers and rubbed me with her long talented fingers. Man, I was ready to shoot off there and then!

Suddenly the elevator stopped and she shrugged off her robe.

I stared at her lean body. She had tiny breasts with pale, extended nipples. "Are we there?" I asked foolishly.

"No, but we soon could be," she replied, pulling at my trousers.

The elevator was small, gave you a bit of claustrophobia, but she managed to get me down to my bare skin.

I must say, in all my dealings with birds I'd never had one behave like *this*.

"Tony, you come up to all my expectations," she muttered. "Now, I'll show you how to do it in an elevator."

Oh, God! What an experience!

Thinking back I didn't get a chance to do much, because she did everything. Of course I rose to the occasion magnificently. I was out of my depth and knew it. I just let her have her way, I wasn't going to blow this setup.

She dug her nails deep into my back and twisted her long white legs around me. She didn't moan or cry out. She muttered, "Screw me, you bastard, keep it hard."

Well, I'd never had any problem doing *that.*

Afterward she was all calm and businesslike. She stood up and put her robe on. She waited for me to struggle into my clothes, and then the elevator took us back to the study.

I was destroyed. I flopped into a chair. She rang a bell, and the butler appeared with tea.

She chatted away in her high-class tinkly voice and who would have thought that a half-hour earlier she'd been raving about in the elevator.

"I want to open a discotheque," she said. "Something different, something chic, somewhere to go that's fun--something mad and exclusive."

"Yes." I was all interest. Here came my big chance.

"You could manage something like that, couldn't you?"

She chatted on about how there was nowhere to go that was chic—"All these places now are filled with scruffy little bores. Don't you think this town needs something different—somewhere for grownups, like Paris has, or Rome?"

Her line of chat killed me. Somewhere for grownups yet! However, I nodded seriously. I was looking for an out from the restaurant—this could be it.

"You start looking for premises, Tony. Money's no problem, my husband will finance the whole thing. We'll pay you a good salary and five per cent of the profits. How's that? Of course, you'll be running the whole show. Does it appeal to you?"

Did it appeal to me? You bet your ass it appealed to me.

She stood up, smoothing her robe. "I have to get dressed now. Start looking and keep in touch." She turned at the door. "Oh, Tony, in the elevator, that was nice, very nice. Let's do it again soon." Then in the same cool voice she added, "The butler will show you out."

It was all too much. This was a real cool lady and a raver to boot. I had a feeling I'd fallen in the right direction.

I set to work, started getting up early in the mornings and hanging around the real estate agents. I saw a lot of lousy joints. I had a feeling for what she wanted and I kept right on looking until I found it. It was a rooftop restaurant that had gone broke—bad neighborhood everyone said, impossible to park—but baby, you get the right doorman and nowhere's impossible. To me, it was just right. Not too big, not too small. Different because instead of creeping down to some cellar you went up and you had windows and a view. I called Fontaine right away, and she came gliding over with a chauffeur in a Silver Cloud Rolls. She loved it, too. We were in business.

We had tea at Fortnum's. I hadn't seen her since the day at her house. She was wearing a silver mink coat and hat, and everyone turned to take another look.

She stared at me with those icy eyes and I knew the look. "Benjamin's home," she said, "but I have another place."

"Well, let's go," I said, gulping down dainty tea sandwiches and feeling pretty good.

She dismissed the chauffeur and we took a cab to a small apartment building in Chelsea. It was one-room luxury, a big bed covered in white fur, rugs, mirrors everywhere, louvered shutters to remove the daylight, and red-tinged lights. A few erotic pictures on the wall, a lot of dirty books and a built-in bookcase next to the bed.

"This is my whore's room," she said with a small, tight smile. I didn't know what to say; I'd never met anyone like her before. She took off her clothes and stretched out on the bed. I fumbled with mine, I mean, well, I was embarrassed!

I finally got them off and started some action. She just lay there very stiff, smiling slightly. Very different from the last time. It was rather exciting, really, took me off guard, so to speak. I mean, I was expecting it to be like the last time.

It didn't take me long before I was through—

wowee! I rolled off her and studied our bodies in the mirrored ceiling.

She said very slowly, "Tony, how would you like to learn to be a good lover?"

I sat up on one elbow and stared at her. Was she kidding? I mean I was all there, you know, I'd never been lacking in *that* department.

As it happens, looking back on it now, I suppose she did teach me a lot. Little tricks she'd picked up in Beirut, Tangier, South America. You name it, she knew it. She was a great teacher, very detailed, I grew to look forward to our little classes more than anything. Of course I was knocking off another bird on the side. Fontaine didn't know about it, but it was useful, gave me a chance to do my homework so I'd be in good shape for Fontaine.

Lana was a stripper, a bit of a scrubber, but a knockout when it came to practicing my lessons. In fact, she added a few ideas of her own. She had the best pair of knockers around, a big full, juicy bird. I mean Fontaine was very classy and all that jazz, but a bit lacking in the tits and ass department. A man likes his steak rare, but he needs his bread and potatoes, too.

Life was really good. I left the restaurant and started organizing the new place. Interior decorators, waiters to find, members' lists, ordering stock. There were a million and one things to do. Fontaine chose the name, Hobo. It was good, although Benjamin offered the suggestion of calling it Fontaine's. She said that would be tasteless and vulgar. She was right. She was usually right.

And so eventually we opened. Big party, lots of publicity, all the right people. They all came, they always turned out in bulk for anything free. Fountaine personally supervised the guest list and I think that's what started the whole thing off—her guest list. It was such a wild mixture—from rock groups to movie stars to high society to hookers (international ones of course)! It was great. It all just happened, and within a few weeks Hobo was *the* place and all of a sudden I was *the* person to know.

It's wild, really, I still sort of expect the bubble to burst. But here I am, Tony Blake—ex-nothing, ex-waiter, now great host, lover, and friend of the stars.

Great me!

# 2

# FONTAINE

I have always enjoyed waking late and breakfasting in bed. Benjamin says it's because bed is my favorite place. He's right, actually. He gets up at the unearthly hour of seven A.M. So I lie awake with my eyes closed and listen to him cough and belch and fart! Delightful! Benjamin Al Khaled in the mornings—I wonder what the society gossip columns would make of an exclusive like that! I've begged him for separate bedrooms, but that's one thing he won't surrender. He likes his nightly ashes hauled, and maybe in the middle of the night if he feels like it. So the communal bedroom stays. It's worth it, he's very very rich. Even I don't know how much he has, millions. He's sixty-one years old and randy as hell.

Bed is delicious. I can lie here and think and relax and not have to do anything. At eleven my maid wakes me. She brings breakfast and the papers, runs my bath and lays out the clothes I tell her to. I can have anything I want. Benjamin will give me anything except actual cash.

We have been married for five years and both of us were married before. His ex-wife is a bitch. Plain and dreary, with two children by him—Alexandra and Ben junior. My ex-husband is somewhere in California now, basking in the sun on the money that Benjamin had to pay him to agree to a divorce. Paul was always lazy. When we married he never did a stroke of work, just lived off my hard-earned modeling money. He *was* rather beautiful though, and very virile. It was a shame to have to divorce him, but I was bored with modeling, and one doesn't grow any younger and there was Benjamin offering me all that divine money. Well, really, I had no choice.

Being married to Benjamin is rather like a part-time job. He works so hard and travels so much that I hardly ever see him. That's why he said I could do the discotheque, somewhere for me to go—"a little interest" as he calls it. "Little interest," indeed. It's making a fortune! Benjamin would have a fit if he knew, he hates me to have any money of my own. He thinks it would make me independent of him. Isn't that silly? As if I would be independent of all his millions.

Benjamin thinks I'm faithful to him. He told me. He thinks that if I'm well looked after at home I won't want any more. For a man of sixty-one he's really very naive, especially since he's away half the time. As if I could be satisfied with that withered old thing!

Fortunately I have arranged my life rather well and I have occasional exciting affairs. In London the current one is Tony. He's rather divine. Very obvious looking, but tremendously sexual. Tall and strong, he has a body rippling with hidden muscles, and a black hairy chest which is *very* exciting. His face is an open invitation to bed. What an innocent he was when I got hold of him, and look at him now. Of course, basically he'll always be a headwaiter, but I think I've improved him beyond recognition.

The first time was a disaster. He had an animal charm, a sexy walk, but that was about all. In bed he had a marvelous body, but he had no skill. For someone so well endowed it was a shame. I thought to myself, he is very attractive in a basic way. If he appeals to me, he would probably appeal to lots of women. That's why I decided to use him in the discotheque. I needed someone, and as it turned out he's just the right person. Of course I know he's having an affair with everyone in sight now, including my best friend Vanessa. He thinks I don't suspect. Isn't that silly? I mean I don't mind, but of course I must pretend not to know, pretend a little touch of jealousy, otherwise his manly pride would be hurt. Vanessa and I laugh about it. "Tony the stud" we call him. It's great fun comparing notes. He thinks he's the best lover in the world. He's not bad, but if he wasn't so well endowed he would be disastrous. Poor conceited Tony.

I'll never forget the first time he came to see me at my house. The clothes he had on—unbelievable! A cheap black silk suit with trousers so tight his pecker shone through like a beacon! I decided I had to take a look. Benjamin was away, so I took him in my lift and enjoyed him there. Well, I mean to say there is nothing more dreary than always doing it on a bed. When I got his clothes off I thought "not bad," but after it was all over I knew there was a lot to teach him.

The best lover I ever had was a great big black Zulu. I was doing a swimsuit layout for one of the glossies deep in the heart of nowhere. We took a break for a cigarette and he grabbed me behind a tree and gave it to me quickly. Delicious! I'll never forget it. His timing was perfect, he brought me to the most beautiful climax ever! Unfortunately we moved to a new location the next day and I never saw him again. I often think about him, usually when Benjamin is sprawled on top of me, huffing and puffing.

Vanessa says Tony is awed by me. Can you imagine! I suppose it's being married to a billionaire and everything. Rather useful, brings people to their knees, lots of respect and all that. Fame, money, and titles, that's all people really care about.

I don't want children. What for? They ruin your figure, give you a lot of boring trouble, then leave you. I don't need children, I don't have what I suppose is called the maternal instinct. Personally, I like being free. My God, my mother never gained any advantages by having me. A woman should be strong, I've seen too many marriages fail because the wife was weak. Vanessa has three children and she never sees them. They live with nanny on the fourth floor and she never goes up there. They might as well be in Siberia, isn't that silly? She doesn't look too bad, a bit saggy. Saved by that pretty face. One day I'm going to tell Tony I know about him and Vanessa. He'd have a fit! He thinks he's being so clever. He's like a little boy, hates being found out. I don't care, as long as he's got enough left for me he can do what he likes. He's really an idiot, a sexy idiot stud. It's that lower-class mentality of his, he'll never change. He's useful though, definitely worth keeping on the leash. And so eager to learn. Always asking me where my handbag came from, and what perfume was I wearing, and who made my clothes.

Think I'll give him a call, pop in before I visit Vanessa . . .

Vanessa was not dressed when I arrived. Her big breasts were flopping about in a blue dressing gown and she was eating toast and honey and reading a gossip column.

It's very important in our circle to see one's name quite often in print. If Vanessa hadn't been very rich she would have been a real slut. I knew that Leonard, her husband, was keeping some little tramp in a flat, but I hadn't told Vanessa—what was the point?

We greeted each other warmly, and I ordered a champagne cocktail from their Filipino houseboy and sat down and relaxed.

"What's new, darling?" Vanessa yawned.

I slipped off my jacket. "Nothing much, just had a little session with the stud."

We both laughed. "Was he in good form today?" Vanessa inquired.

I have a feeling she has a secret crush on Tony, offhand as she may try to be.

"Yes," I replied. "When is he ever not?"

Vanessa was a bit bored at that. She had to wait for Tony to approach her, *I* had a far different relationship with him.

The houseboy brought my cocktail It was cold and delicious, a good champagne cocktail really sets you up for the day.

"What are you wearing tonight?" I asked.

Vanessa shrugged. "I haven't really thought."

Hadn't really thought indeed. I planned my outfits months ahead. No wonder she always looked such a mess.

We chatted a while longer and then I went off to the hairdresser's to prepare for what I supposed would be a dreary evening with Benjamin's darling daughter.

She dislikes me and I can't stand her, but of course Benjamin fails to see this

At least I would wear my new full-length white mink; Vanessa would love it. I have no doubt she will shortly appear in a bad copy—she copies everything I have, but it invariably just doesn't suit her to wear my style We are completely different types.

Oh, well, roll on fun evening!

# 3

# TONY

Tonight's going to be good. Two big parties in town and everyone will be coming along after. Fontaine nearly caught me today. Fast asleep in bed with this bird—Janet something or other—and her ladyship phones. "I'm coming over." Charming!

Wake up Janet.

She complains, horrible whiny voice, long sloppy black hair, ugh! I must have been well stoned. She struggles complaining into a dress hardly long enough to cover her ass, nice ass. I shove her out the front door, and five minutes later Fontaine comes wafting in. I hardly had time to hide the sheets!

Sometimes she's like a witch, very cold. "I

have to go to the hairdresser's," she announces, stepping out of her Rhavis skirt, Gucci shoes and Dior stockings. At times I hate her, I'm not a machine. She remains standing with her suit jacket still on, her hair hidden in a mink turban. She leans obscenely against the wall. She wants it standing up. I think of her husband. She looks like a high-fashion model top half and a dirty photograph bottom half. The thought excites me and I manage to accommodate her. Oh, God, I can imagine the scene if she'd caught me this morning!

She dresses briskly. Her legs are getting thinner, she diets too much. "I'll see tonight," she says, zipping up her skirt. "Keep my table for seven. We have a French diplomat and his wife with us." Then she was gone, leaving a cloud of Hermes' Calèche.

It was a good thing when it started. Fontaine Khaled and all that jazz. But she's kinky, she's definitely kinky, and I don't want to be used the way she uses me. Her whore's room and her strange preferences.

What about her old man? Poor guy, he's working his ass off while she's handing out the action. Never trust a woman, that's what I say. Now I've got all the crumpet I want. High class crumpet galore. But she's got me by the balls. Hobo is hers. If I want out of screwing her, then I'm out, period. It's not really fair. I built the whole place up, worked my ass off until five every morning, and all I get is peanuts compared to what the joint is making—and I've yet to see my five per cent of the profits. I have no contract, nothing. I just work for her. She's a pretty cool bitch—a pretty clever bitch.

"Franco, bring me a Scotch." Franco's a great headwaiter. Probably I could grab him if I left here and opened up somewhere else. But with what? I've got no bread. People have offered to back me in a new place—women—it would be same scene all over again. I was casting my eye around for a guy to promote a new joint, one of the rich Greeks would do. Got one in mind, but I'll have to play it cool, make it seem like his idea.

"Hallo, Tony darling." This bird threw her arms around me, I swear I'd never seen her before.

"How are you?" I said beaming with pleasure, winking. The well-known Blake charm churned forth.

"I'm fine. This is Chicky and this is Robin and this is Henry." Three nonentities strained forward to give me greeting. The evening was starting.

There are certain regulars who always congregate at the top table. It's called the top table because it's at the top of the room in the best position for seeing everything, and it's where I sit, *when* I sit, which is about twice a night. I always make sure it's available for any visiting celebrities in case there's nowhere else. The regulars can always be shuffled around. If I have a date, she sits there. Oh, I'm allowed to have dates as long as it's not the same girl too often. After all, they just sit there by themselves all night.

The regulars are all guys, a varied selection, my friends. There's Sammy—small, wiry, dark-haired. A hat manufacturer, crumpet mad—always chatting up different birds. Likes them tall. I should really get him and Fontaine together, but she thinks he's revolting, and he says she's a rich old bag. Any female over twenty is an old bag to him. Sammy's a sweet guy, but a lot of people don't understand him.

Then there's Franklin—quiet, young, good-looking and shy. Sits there drinking Coca-Cola all night. We all reckon he's a virgin.

Next Hal—an American promoter, constantly stoned, a wow with rich old widows. Fortyish, attractive if you like the Dean Martin type. He has a big heart; every bit of honest bread he makes he sends to his kid brother in New Jersey, and that's the only thing he doesn't brag about.

Lastly, Massey, a singer. Good-looking in a black-is-beautiful way. Great dancer.

When there's nothing better to do and if none

of us have dates, we sit there and discuss the talent. "I'd like to screw that!" is a constant cry from our table.

Fontaine hates them all. "Why do you always have that motley group around?" she questions But they pay, so there's nothing she can do.

They all suspect about Fontaine and me, but no one actually knows. I like the regulars. They're a good group of guys.

Franklin came in first tonight. With a girl, surprise, surprise His father is a big guy in the film business. The bird he was with was definitely too hot for him, probably thought he'd put in a good word with Dad. She had those pouty lips and jaded eyes that all would-be movie stars have. Too much screwing and not enough fresh air! Franklin was treating her like a lady, all proper and polite. He's a nice kid, but a schmuck. Treat them rough if you want to lay them. She had lots of long thick reddish hair, and she gave me the well-known come on look.

"Janine James—Tony Blake," Franklin said. "Janine's over here doing a film."

"Hi," she simpered.

Ugh, sometimes American girls turn me off, that horrible nasal twang. I gave her my angry, knowing stare. That usually gets them. She responded with what I took to be a sexy look.

Poor Franklin, he didn't have a chance with this one.

The next of the regulars to bounce in was Sammy—friendly, Cockney, pussy-crazy Sammy. As luck would have it he had no date, and he immediately launched into a line of chat with Janine. Franklin sat silently, I could see it was going to be one of those nights.

Fontaine's usual table was next to ours. I had explained to her a hundred times that she couldn't have the top table because it was the only table that could be made easily available in an emergency. This bugged her, but she settled for the next best. After all, she certainly wasn't there every night. Maybe six nights in a row, then not at all for two or three weeks while she was on her travels. The places she went made me dizzy. Benjamin Khaled had his own private jet, which was useful. She never came in with less than five or six people. She had this girl friend Vanessa, blond, pretty, a bit plump, but with huge bouncy knockers. Married to the son of the owner of a very famous chain store. Worth a fortune. Got three kids. Vanessa was a mess. She idolized Fontaine and copied her faithfully. It was only fair that I should screw her too. She practically begged me. I went to her house one afternoon while hubby was at the office and the kids were out with nanny. I don't think she knows about me and

Fontaine. Anyway she promised she wouldn't tell anybody about us. I hope to God she doesn't. It's all very risky. Anyway she's a lousy lay, but those unbelievable tits. I could just stay playing with them for hours. They smother you, all big and soft, very mumsy. Vanessa is usually in Fontaine's group, with or without hubby, who isn't bad—a lot better than Benjamin. I hear he's got a girl tucked away in a neat little flat. In my business you get to hear most things.

Fontaine and party made the grand entrance about one-thirty. She was covered with white mink to the ground. Her hair was piled high and secured with gleaming diamonds. Husband was by her side, short and fat. She looked fantastic. Who would have thought that in the morning she had been leaning against my bedroom wall with her pubics on show! I had an insane desire to shout out "I've had that!" but instead I went into the whole greeting routine. All the kisses and nice-to-see-yous and all that bullshit. Vanessa and hubby were naturally present. She looked her usual pretty mess. Wispy hair, boobies flopping in a chiffon dress. I gave her an unseen tweak on the nipple when I kissed her cheek. She blushed, I shook hands with hubby. "How's Veronica?" I was tempted to say. Veronica was his girl friend.

They had an elderly French couple with them, and a youngish man and a girl. She stood back from the others and was quite obviously embarrassed by all the loud greetings. She was plainly dressed in comparison, a simple woolen dress, slightly too long, and a single strand of pearls. She had long, shining auburn hair pulled straight back and secured with a plain pearl slide. Very little make-up—in fact she wasn't that pretty—but there was something about her that gave me a jolt I could feel right in the pit of my stomach. She had these wide brown very innocent eyes that stared at me with slight contempt. She certainly wasn't some little ding-a-ling obsessed by who to lay next, or how short her skirt could get. She was quite young, about seventeen or eighteen. All in the space of seconds I knew that I had to have this one. This one was special.

They were all sitting down. Wasn't anyone going to introduce me? Fontaine was busy ordering champagne, her cool aquamarine eyes darting around to see who was in. She waved at a few people and then Vanessa's husband took her off to dance. If there's one thing Fontaine's lousy at, it's dancing. It's good to know there is at least one thing she can't do. She's got no rhythm, sort of jerks around like a skinny puppet.

I smiled at the guy with the auburn-haired girl and extended my hand. "I'm Tony Blake," I said, very friendly like.

The girl didn't even glance at me. She stared off into the middle distance, looking bored. The guy was a creep. Square suit, short back and sides, a real nothing.

Benjamin joined in, "Oh, Tony, don't you know Peter Lincoln Smith?"

The name rang a bell. I had met his father several times. He owned half of London.

"And this is my daughter Alexandra," he finished proudly, "just arrived home from Switzerland today."

His daughter Alexandra! My mouth must have hung open for at least five minutes. His daughter!

She threw me a sulky "How do you do."

The French couple butted in then, and I had to chat with them. It seemed their daughter came in all the time and they had heard lots about me. Their daughter was an ugly little blond nympho who wore Paco Rabanne dresses and thought she was the knockout of all times. I hadn't actually been there, but Sammy had, and his verdict was thumbs down.

Benjamin was now urging the creep to dance with Alexandra. She was blushing and saying she didn't want to dance. Peter Lincoln Smith was caught in the middle and didn't know what to do, whether to please Daddy or daughter. Daddy won, and a reluctant Alexandra was led off to the dance floor. There were hints of a great body. The dress wasn't showing anything, but it was there, hidden underneath.

I didn't know what to do, I was caught up with this girl, don't know why. I hadn't even spoken to her, she was probably a spoiled rich bitch. I fancied her like crazy. Man, this was going to be tricky, dare I take the risk?

Fontaine came back to the table, breathless and slightly hot in all that white mink. The whole room had seen it, so she slipped it off, revealing a black body-molding backless sheath. She certainly knew how to show herself off.

I took myself back to the regulars' table and ordered a stiff Scotch. Massey had arrived with a thin angular model called Suki. Her hair was cropped close to her head, her skirt close to her ass, and she wore weird white makeup with huge clownlike eyes.

Massey was his usual cool self. "Hey, man," he said sitting down beside Sammy, "what's the action tonight?"

"Same old action, everything swinging," I replied.

He was wearing a white suit, very smart. I thought I might get myself a white suit.

I spied Alexandra on the dance floor. Amongst all the ravers she stood quietly holding her boy friend at arms' length and doing a sort of nothing shuffle.

I grabbed Suki and took her off to dance, edging my way closer near to Alexandra. The only reaction she gave was a slightly incredulous look at Suki. Shit! What could I do to make the rich bitch notice me?

Suki was a very stylized dancer, religiously studied every new step, and wouldn't be caught dead doing anything that was out. She and Massey made a very together couple. Me—I did a sort of wild shake and that was it.

"I bet this is different from Switzerland," I yelled above the din of the music, an inane grin on my face.

Alexandra just ignored me. Either that or she didn't hear me.

Suki said. "What?"

"Nothing," I muttered, dragging her back to the table.

Carla Cassini, an Italian actress, was making her entrance surrounded by three attractive men.

"Wowee," Sammy whistled through his teeth. "How about that?"

She was beautiful, with black hair, olive skin, a body edging on being plump, but ending up merely voluptuous. Her new movie had just opened in town. Something about a peasant girl who gets raped by an army. I could understand the army!

I hurried over to give greetings, shaking hands warmly, meeting crystal-clear green eyes, a throaty accented voice. Ordinarily I would have become Charlie Charm, dancing attendance. but tonight my mind was elsewhere. I saw she got a good table, and left her with the three guys.

Miss Rich Bitch was sitting at her table. Peter was being led off to dance by Fontaine. I nipped in quickly. Vanessa was dancing with her husband and Benjamin was talking to the French couple. I sat down next to Alexandra and we both stared off into space. She was drinking plain orange juice. "How do you like it?" I asked.

"How do I like what?" Her voice was soft and very precise.

"The club." I waved an expansive arm around.

"Very nice," she said, stifling a yawn. I noticed her nails were cut short and painted a buff color. Most of the girls or women I knew had either long red talons, or short clipped bitten ones.

"Would you like to dance?"

"No thank you."

No, thank you, indeed! Most girls would give their false eyelashes to dance with me! We sat there with nothing else to say until Fontaine and Peter returned.

The club was filling to capacity. The music was getting louder and louder. Time to take off the records and put on the group. Time to circulate around some tables, give them the chat. Time to give the waiters a blast.

I got up. Silly little cow, she wasn't even that

pretty, and man, like I could have the prettiest. I grabbed my Scotch, gulped it down and wandered around the joint. People liked me to sit down at their table, it showed they were really "in." I tell you this is such a phony business; maybe that's why I dug Alexandra sitting there so bored and unimpressed.

I joined the table of the Italian star. She was with her "producer"—fat, good-looking, didn't speak a word of English; an English actor; and his stunt-man boy friend. Carla Cassini was very lovely, with this incredibly throaty accent. The producer kept a firm hand on her thigh, but she winked at me and flirted, safe in the knowledge that he didn't understand one word.

"You are veree attractive," she purred. "Such a lovely body, but no money, huh? It ees beeg shame." She laughed a deep sexy chuckle. She was a smart cookie.

I asked her to dance, she shook her head. "Ee is veree veree jealous," she indicated the producer, "ee don't like me to dance with other man."

Nobody wanted to dance with me, it just wasn't my night.

Suddenly Franco rushed over, stared bug-eyed at Carla and whispered something in my ear. It seemed some black chick had come in wearing a topless dress, and what was he to do? Should he ask her to cover up, or what? He pointed her out, she had just sat down, and the top of her dress, which was all fringe, parted as she moved, revealing firm dark brown breasts. It was tantalizing—now you see them, now you don't. The guy she was with was old, suited, obviously out on a jaunt. She was a wild chick called Molly Mandy, a part-time dress designer. What the hell, there was no law against topless dresses. I told Franco to leave her be.

A few people had noticed and a lot of staring was going on; then she got up to dance and staring really began. The old guy didn't care, he got up there with her, proud as punch. She started on a slow shake, titties hardly moving, then suddenly she started to go, and the fringe swung, and the titties swung and baby, *she* swung.

Everyone stopped dancing and made a hand-clapping circle around them. The guys all loved it; some of the birds looked a bit flustered. I saw Fontaine rush over to the side of the dance floor with Vanessa to get a better look.

It was a wild scene. Then the Greeks joined in, threw some glasses to start off, then a couple of them shouldered the old guy out of the way and started dancing with Molly. One of their girl friends, not to be outdone, ripped off her blouse, unhooked her bra and joined the scene. Everyone cheered.

The time had come to stop it, otherwise we'd

get the police in. Charming! I pushed my way through the crowd just a little too late. One of the mad Greek shipowners had grabbed hold of a brown tit, and the old guy attempted to punch him and ended up flat on his back.

A lot of screaming started, but Franco had his waiters in there fast, the old guy was carried out, the Greeks were persuaded to go back to their table, and Molly sat down at our table saying, "Shit, man, what's all the fuss?"

It was action like this that made Hobo the only place in town.

I glanced over to Fontaine's table. She was just sitting down, laughing. Alexandra and escort had gone, probably left during all the confusion. Just as well.

"Hey, Molly, baby, don't come here like that again," I said.

She smiled at me, rows of white pearly teeth plus a few gold fillings. "What's the matter, Tony sweetheart, don't you like my boobies?" She shook her shoulders and the fringe parted giving me a big eyeful.

"You know I like them, but not in here. You'll cause a riot. Come on, I'll take you back to find your boy friend."

She made a face, "Man, that old fart's out cold. I feel like some fun tonight."

I was getting irritated. What did she expect,

to tag onto me? I didn't even fancy her. I looked to Sammy, but he was busy chatting up Janine

I took a grip on her arm and led her to the reception area; the old guy was laid out in the office at the back. He was just coming to when we got there.

"I'll come back. Isn't it about time you and I had a scene?"

I gave her a shove toward the old trout and got out of there. I think it was the gold fillings that turned me off.

Fontaine summoned me with the imperial wave when I was back inside. I knew the gesture well—she raised one long thin arm high and sort of clicked her fingers at me. Charming! Sort of a—come here serf!

I went. After all she was the boss.

"Tell us all about it," she said, excitement gleaming in her eyes. The others all leaned forward too, anxious to hear the story. "Who was that pathetic little man with her?" Fontaine went on "I mean, really, they made a ridiculous couple." She gave me a sharp kick under the table, her signal that she wanted me to ask her to dance.

I obliged I hated dancing with her. Talk about looking ridiculous—is there anything more ridiculous than an elegant looking lady jumping and squirming around like a seventeen-year-old? Especially when she's got no sense of rhythm. I gave my secret signal to Flowers, the disc jockey, to put on a slow record; he's the best DJ in town. A tall thin black guy with freak-out hair and pale blue eyes. Usually stoned out of his mind. But he can feel a room like I can feel a woman. He launched into a medley of Tony Bennett, making a face; he was strictly a Motown man.

Fontaine held me tight. "Did you touch her?" she asked, licking silver-coated lips.

"Did I touch who?"

"Oh, you know who." I ignored that. Fontaine had a poor opinion of anyone who wasn't in her set.

She was dancing very close. I glanced over at her husband. He was talking with the French couple.

"Hello, Tone," a girl greeted me. She was dancing alongside us. I smiled at her. Fontaine dug me in the ribs and said with an amused smile, "You love it, don't you, all these little dollies after you."

I must admit I did love it.

Wouldn't you?

# 4

# ALEXANDRA

It's great to be home.

Madelaine and I flew back together. Her father and her brother Michael met us at the airport. I've known her brother for ages. We were all children together, but lately he has become so attractive.

I daren't tell Maddy what I think of him because she wouldn't understand. I mean him being her brother and everything, she most likely sees him in a different light. We always discuss boys together, not that there was too much chance in Switzerland. Our school was run like a convent. However, Maddy had this huge crush on the school gardener. I used to unlock the hall window at night and she'd sneak out to meet him. We'd probably both have been expelled if we'd been found out. He was quite old, about thirty, and they used to neck and once she let him take her sweater off *and* her bra. But she said he went a bit berserk after that and used to try all sorts of things, so she didn't meet him any more. It was just as well, because I didn't think he was much at all.

Anyway, here we are out of school at last!

Madelaine and I have a plan. She's going to work on her parents and I'm going to work on my mother and we're going to share a flat. We decided Chelsea was the best place, sort of swinging and everything.

After all, I've been seventeen two whole months now, I'm practically old! And nothing has ever happened to me—nothing!

We went back to Maddy's house, it's in Virginia Water, and she's always lived there, with both parents. My parents are divorced. We were all so happy before, and my mother is great fun. Very sensible. I wish she wasn't so sensible, then perhaps she would have held onto him. I must admit that Fontaine, his new wife, is quite glamorous. She hates me, I can tell. Not that I care because I can't *stand* her, and fortunately I don't have to see them very much, only on occasions like tonight when I'm on my way home from school.

Tomorrow morning I'm getting the train down to my mother's house near Newmarket.

"What are you wearing tonight?" Maddy came into the room wrapped in a towel. She always took ages in the bath. I had been waiting to get in the bathroom for half an hour.

"I'm not going to dress up," I replied. Actually I didn't have anything to dress up in if I'd wanted to, because we mostly lived in sweaters and skirts in Switzerland. Both Madelaine and I had to get ourselves new wardrobes. Our school clothes were awful and old-fashioned.

"I don't blame you," Maddy said. "I certainly wouldn't get dressed up for *her*, either."

We shared a loathing for Fontaine, although Maddy has never met her, but knows all about her from me.

I bathed, brushed my hair, and put on the cleanest dress I could find in my jumbled suitcase.

"Have a glorious time," Maddy said when I was ready. "See you later." I was coming back to stay the night.

I went downstairs to find Mr. Newcombe. He was going to a business dinner in London.

Oh, good! Michael's coming too. He's very good-looking, tall, with lovely, longish hair. He lives in London. I hope when Maddy and I get our flat in town we'll see lots of him.

He sat in the front of the car with his father, and I was in the back, so there wasn't much chance for talking on the way.

My father lives in a ghastly big house in Belgravia. It has a lot of white statues balanced about outside. and inside it's huge and not at all comfortable. There is even an indoor swimming pool which is in a sort of glass room, all dark and depressing, with hundreds of vines and plants growing around it. I loathe it.

I said good-bye to Mr. Newcombe. Michael smiled at me.

I said, "See you soon."

Maybe he likes me too. Maddy was always talking about how he has lots of girl friends, maybe I could be one of them, or *the* one. I mused on this as the butler let me in and took my coat.

Fontaine came bearing down on me. "Alexandra, darling, how wonderful to see you." She kissed me on the cheek. I knew she was only doing it for Daddy's sake.

He hugged me. He seems to have grown shorter and older. Suddenly I felt a warmth toward him and I hugged him back. Oh, if only he'd stayed with Mummy! Everyone knew Fontaine just loved him for his money.

"We're going to have a lovely evening," my father said. "How was school? Tell me all about it."

We sat together on the sofa, and I wanted to cry because he looked so old and tired. I had seen him four months before and he had looked fine, but now—what had she done to him?

"Are you well, Daddy?"

"Of course I'm well. Working very hard, but that's what I like. I was never one for sitting about." He glanced over at Fontaine, but she was taking no notice of us. She was sipping champagne and reading a fashion magazine. "How's your mother?"

"I haven't been home yet, but I spoke to her tonight and she sounds fine. She said she just got a letter from Ben and he's having a marvelous time."

My brother Ben is at a university in America.

"Wonderful woman, your mother, very strong . . ." He trailed off. I could still remember the day Mummy told us he was leaving. She hadn't cried or anything, but I knew he was breaking her heart. My mother is a pretty woman, about fifty. When she was young, she was gorgeous. I knew that she had married my father long before he was rich.

"I'll give Mummy your love," I said, and wondered if that was the right thing to say. But it must have been all right because he just smiled and patted me on the knee.

"I'm going to come and live in London," I blurted out. "I'm going to share a flat with Madelaine and get a job."

"When did you decide all this?"

"Well, Maddy and I have been thinking about it for ages. Actually it's not all set yet, but I've written off for three jobs and I've got interviews next week, and Maddy's got two flats to see."

My father frowned. "But if you want to come to London you can live here. You don't need to get a job. Fontaine and I would be more than delighted to have you here."

"No, Daddy, you don't understand. I'm eighteen now and I know at twenty-one I'll have money from my Trust. Well that's why I want to keep myself; sort of support myself for a few years. I don't want to be just a rich man's daughter. I want to think for myself and work for myself, and then at twenty-one I'll be ready to accept the responsibility of my money. I don't want to 'come out' and be a deb. I want a few years as just an ordinary girl."

There! I'd said it. The speech I'd had prepared for my mother.

Father beamed. "That's my girl," he said, "that's my little girl. But I could help you and find a nice job. You could take your choice."

"No, Daddy."

Some more people arrived, and my father joined Fontaine in greeting them.

"Alexandra, I want you to meet Peter Lincoln Smith. He's kindly agreed to escort you this evening."

My face burned. *Kindly* agreed to escort me! Oh, my father was so embarrassing. I didn't want to be fixed up, it was so awful and old-fashioned, and my father hadn't even mentioned it to me.

Peter Lincoln Smith had a mean thin mouth and a limp handshake. I didn't like him, and I don't think he liked me.

There were two other couples, much older people. We had a long, dull dinner at Annabel's. I wished I was with Michael.

Fontaine never stopped talking all night. I really don't know how my father can stand her, she's so loud.

Afterward they all wanted to go to a discotheque and Peter and I had to go too. I don't think we had exchanged more than six words all evening.

I felt embarrassed trailing in behind Fontaine. Everyone stared. At one point the manager sat down and tried to be nice to me, for Daddy's sake, I suppose.

I felt very tired. It had been a busy day and I had the long ride back to Virginia Water. I asked Peter if he'd mind putting me in a taxi.

There was some commotion on the dance floor and Fontaine had rushed over to see what it was. So I said good night to Daddy and thankfully left.

Peter had a red MG in which he had driven me to the club. "I'll run you home," he said.

"Oh, no, it's much too far and much too

late." I didn't want to face another hour of Peter's company.

"Nonsense," he said, suddenly linking his arm in mine. "No traffic at this time of night. It won't take long."

So I was stuck. I climbed in and we set off in silence. Peter drove fast and I leaned back in the seat. I soon fell asleep. I must have slept for ages, because when I awoke we were parked in a country lane, and Peter was kissing me.

I didn't know what to do, he had taken me by surprise, and I didn't want to offend him. After all he had driven me all this way. So I sat quietly while he kissed me, waiting for the right moment to push him away. Suddenly I felt his hand on my breast. Well, I certainly wasn't going to just sit there now. I moved his hand away. "Please stop that, Peter," I said firmly.

But he didn't, and soon I found myself really struggling. His hands were everywhere. "Don't fight me," he said, as I managed to push his hands away again, "just lie back and enjoy it."

I hated him! He had one hand up my skirt now, and I swung my arm at his head with all the force I could muster.

He stopped at once, clutching his mouth where my blow had landed. "You little bitch!" he exclaimed in surprise.

I jumped out of the car and ran off into the

night. It was awfully dark, it wasn't a main road at all, and I had no idea where I was. I heard a car. It was Peter's, headlights full on. He was coming to find me.

I didn't know what to do. Should I duck down and hide, and hope he wouldn't see me? Or should I climb in his car and demand he take me home?

It was cold and spitting rain. I was completely lost. I stood quietly by the side of the road, with dignity I hoped. The car stopped beside me and Peter leaned over from the driving seat and flung open the door.

"It's all right. I'm not going to rape you," he said as though reading my thoughts. "Get in."

I climbed into the car. The least he could do was apologize.

As it happened we were only about five minutes from Maddy's house, and we both maintained a stony silence on the short dirve. I climbed out as soon as he stopped the car. "Good night," I said coldly.

"Good-by, cock teaser!" he yelled, and drove away.

# 5

# FONTAINE

We left Hobo and once in the privacy of our bedroom I flopped on the bed exhausted. What a day!

Benjamin announced he had to leave for Paris the next afternoon. Did I want to come? Well, I wanted to come, but not to Paris. I decided I might pop over to New York to our flat for a few days. I adored the shops over there and I supposed I should visit Ray. He is an adorable hairdresser whom Benjamin has set up in his own salon there. I haven't spent time with Ray for ages. A few days with him might be fun.

Benjamin was pulling at my dress. He knew I hated that. I got up quickly and he backed away. Oh, poor old thing, I'd frightened him. He was always frightened I'd say no—but of course I never did.

I peeled off the dress and hung it up carefully, then I lay flat on the bed, the way he liked me to, and waited for him.

I closed my eyes and thought about Tony and Ray and Paul and it wasn't too bad. In fact, if he wasn't so fast it might not be bad at all.

He washed himself after, a habit that drives me to distraction. I took off my make-up and put on my sleep mask. He was reading now. Oh, for separate bedrooms. What a joy! Sex with Benjamin is so boring, and yet I suppose it is worth it. After all I love having beautiful clothes and jewels, being envied and stared at. I suppose I always knew that I was destined for this kind of life.

I was a very plain child, with a very plain mother and a bastard of a father who made my mother's life a misery. Felicity Brown of Bournemouth. I grew up very quietly, went to the best girls' school, decided I would like to be a vet, and knew nothing about sex except what the other girls whispered. All nice little English girls want to be vets, it's a part of our tradition—well it was then anyway. At sixteen I was allowed on my first outing with a young man—none of this "raped at thirteen" business in my past. He was nineteen, the local doctor's son, and a nice quiet boy. We got along fine, held hands, had a few furtive kisses and decided to get married. I was a good, chaste Bournemouth virgin, engaged to be married, with a sweet marquisette ring, and stars in my dull little eyes. We decided, with the help of our middle-class parents, that we would marry when he was twenty-one and I was eighteen. My future was cut out and planned. He went off to finish his medical studies and I enrolled in all sorts of activities, such as sewing and cooking classes. I really didn't know any other boys and I thought I loved Mark. What a situation! I had no idea what love was all about.

At cooking class I met a girl called Marcia. She was pregnant and unmarried, and people whispered about her. My mother called her "fast" and "shocking," and my father said it was a disgrace she was allowed to join the cooking class. But join she did, and she was the first breath of fresh air I had encountered in all my nearly seventeen years. We became friendly and I told her all about Mark and my plans.

"What's he like in bed?" she asked.

I looked at her blankly.

"Oh, no," she started to laugh, "don't tell me you haven't?"

I had to admit that I hadn't. What's more I wasn't going to, because it wasn't what nice girls did, was it?

That made her laugh even more, and then she got very serious and said, "How on earth can you marry someone if you don't know if you like each other in bed? It's very important, you *must* do it."

Of course she was no walking advertisement for sex, with her belly swollen out and no visible husband, but I did think she was right, I *should* try it.

I waited anxiously for Mark to come home on holiday, half excited, half terrified at what I planned to do.

He was allowed to borrow his father's car, and we went to a film and he held my hand and afterward we went to one of the big hotels and had dinner.

It's very difficult when you're a nice quiet virgin to suggest that your equally nice quiet fiancé make love to you, especially when he's never attempted anything along those lines.

I said, "Let's drive down to the beach, it's such a lovely night."

"Felicity, I'm tired."

"Please, Mark." I was determined to get the deed done.

"All right," he agreed reluctantly.

We parked somewhere along the front and sat there. He made no movement toward me.

After a few moments of silence, I said, "Mark,

if we're going to get married don't you think we should get to know each other?"

"What are you talking about, Felicity?" he replied crossly.

I moved closer to him, "You know what I mean."

He was genuinely shocked and pushed me away, "If I want that type of girl, there's plenty around."

I was very excited by this time, the first moment in my life I had been sexually excited, and Mark, the man in my life, was pushing me away. I was furious.

He drove me home in silence and I refused ever to see him again.

The next night, still determined to find out what sex was all about, I went to a local coffee bar, and there met a tall leather-jacketed boy called Ted. I had seen Ted before around town, and I decided that he would do to initiate me into the mysteries of life. We started to talk and when he invited me for a walk I accepted readily.

We strolled along making our way toward the beach, and then he grabbed hold of me, kissed me, pushed his hands up my skirt and we both fell down on the sand. I was ready for him without any preliminaries. He forced his way into me and the pain was exquisite and I clung to him and begged him for more, and as he was finished and went limp I wouldn't let him go. He was trying to get away and I was hanging on to him. It was wonderful. We fought silently and he called me a bitch and said I was hurting him! *Me* hurting *him*—that was a delightful statement.

A new Felicity Brown had emerged. I loved it! I tried everyone and everything. A whole new life had opened up for me and soon Bournemouth wasn't big enough and I left for London. My father by this time was pleased to see me go. My mother shed a few tears I think.

I arrived in London, tall, skinny, with mousy hair, but plenty to offer. And by the time I was twenty-two I was Fontaine—top model. Beautiful—a few changes here and there—a girl with London at her feet.

I was making lots of money and lots of men, and then I met my first husband, Paul. He was very attractive. Lean and lazy with smoky green eyes and a beautiful body. He was a sometime male model, sometime actor, but mostly he just enjoyed living off some lady. He was divine in bed. His gymnastics nearly matched up to mine. He was the first man who really satisfied me and saw to it that I stayed satisfied.

So one day we got married amid a blaze of flashbulbs, and he sat back while I worked, and life went on. He gambled and drank and was unfaithful, but we stayed together, because I suppose I must have loved him.

Everyone told me I was mad, but there was still a little bit of Felicity Brown left in me somewhere, and I wanted my marriage to work.

At twenty-nine I looked in the mirror and took stock. I had been a top model for seven years and that's a long time to have been at the top in any profession. How much longer could it last? Paul used up all my money, soon I would be thirty, and how many more magazine covers lay ahead?

Also I was exhausted. Modeling is not an easy job as people seem to think, it's backbreaking work, a constant grind of hairdressers, make-ups, blinding hot lights, and anatomically impossible poses.

I certainly wasn't faithful to Paul any more; after six months of marriage we had both agreed it was ridiculous to confine ourselves to each other. As a matter of fact, we had rather a lot of fun with "group parties." Very interesting.

I finally decided Paul was a luxury that would have to go, and I cast my eyes around for someone more substantial to take his place.

I met Benjamin in St. Moritz. I was doing a fur show there for one day and he was with his unbelievably dreary wife and two ghastly children. We met in a group and I knew who he was. We managed a few words alone. "Can I see you in London?" he asked. He reached a little past my shoulder in height. I gave him my phone number.

It took exactly five weeks for him to offer to divorce his wife. I played my game very carefully, gave him everything but, and I had him mad for it. There's a ghastly expression Tony uses—"I'm hot for you, baby"—and that just about sums up how Benjamin felt.

It was no problem getting rid of Paul. Benjamin paid, and Paul took. Benjamin's wife was also easy. She agreed to divorce him with no argument. Of course she got a fortune and also the children. We have never spoken, but I am obliged to see Ben junior and Alexandra sometimes. They are really very dreary. Young Benjamin is twenty and an even shorter version of his father. Alexandra is just plain, no sparkle, like her mother I suppose.

So that's my story. Benjamin and I got married—once more in a blaze of flashbulbs—and we honeymooned on a new yacht he bought for the occasion.

He buys me whatever I want, I have my occasional stud and I'm happy—I suppose. Whatever happened to Felicity Brown?

# 6

## TONY

Sammy said, "Whatcha dancing with that old bag for?"

Sammy Schmuck! What did he know about class?

"I mean I know she owns the place, but—"

"I think she's fantastic," Janine interrupted, "really fantastic. Did you see that coat she had on?"

"What's a coat if there's nothing but skin and bone underneath?" Sammy chuckled at his own joke. "Now that Italian number's not bad, nice pair of boobies."

I should remark that Sammy has no conversation except about women. We have all heard clinical descriptions of every bird he's ever laid.

'Come on, darling, I'll do you a favor," Sammy dragged Janine off to the packed dance floor.

Franklin looked miserable. "Listen, long face," I said, "that's not for you. Let Sammy have her, she's a pig."

Massey said, "I've got a beautiful little bird for you. Suki's sister—wouldn't she be great for Franklin?"

Suki nodded, her wide clownlike eyes sparkled. "She's only fifteen, but lovely."

I had heard it all before. Everyone was always fixing Franklin up, but nothing ever worked out. He was too shy to make it with a bird. To get Franklin laid was one of our group projects. He would sit and listen to all our chat about women and agree with us when we told him he should blow his cherry, but nothing ever happened.

The evening was at its peak.

The place was so jammed that some tables' occupants had to take it in shifts to dance because there wasn't room for them all to sit down at the same time. It was always dodgy dancing at this time anyway. For one thing the tiny dance floor was so jam packed you couldn't move, and for another you took the risk of losing your seat altogether.

I looked around with satisfaction. It was one of the more star-packed nights. There was a good sprinkling of top talent from most professions.

The Must, the current top rock group, were all present. Long hair, flowered shirts, beads and bells. They were nice boys, stoned out of their heads, but harmless with their flaxen-haired girl friends who all looked the same. It's funny thing how in the rock world it's important to all be on the same wavelength—you know—the long hair bit. They all look like out of the same mold. They try to be different from everyone else and bingo—there you go—all the same.

More people were crowding in, I got up and did the greeting bit. I wandered around a few tables having a Scotch here and a Scotch there. The world was starting to buzz. I could fancy something cuddly. Fontaine had left me with a sour taste in my mouth. As a matter of fact, I could fancy Vanessa. But that was impossible, there she was with hubby. I must remember to give her a ring, sneak in while nanny and the kiddies were out!

I kept on thinking of Miss Rich Bitch—she was so different from other birds, she had this kind of aura of class which I dug. I wondered if I'd see her again. Probably not, she looked like she hated it here.

Flowers grabbed hold of me—"Got to see you, man," his eyes were distorted and nervous.

He was flying on pot, probably needed more bread, that was always his problem. He was living with Tina, our Swedish receptionist. What a couple they made—he, dark and wild, she, white and quiet. There was a song there somewhere!

I lent him five pounds, listened to his bullshit about how grateful he was, and made a mental note to get it back from his next week's salary—otherwise I'd never see it again.

Miss Italian Movie Star and party were leaving. "Bye-bye Tonee," she purred slowly through pearly white teeth, "not long before we shall meet again, huh?"

I loved her voice, it was a real turn-on. "Yeah," I gave her the sincere stare. All the Italian waiters were going mad, hovering around to get a closer look. "S'long, Tony, old boy," the actor said. "Bye, Tone," the stunt man said. They all wanted to know me, be my friend. The Italian producer muttered some Italian, gave me a dirty look, gripped Carla by the arm, and they were gone. Good, I quickly had Franco put a visiting senator and party at their table.

So the evening reached its peak and slowly around two-thirty it started to thin out and by three-thirty only the super swingers and the odd-balls were left. Franklin said he was going and Janine said she wanted to stay, and they argued quietly, and then he left.

I caught him at the door. "Listen kid, we'll get you a date with Suki's sister. O.K.?" He shrugged. A waiter came at him with his check and I grabbed. "The Cokes are on me tonight," I said.

"Thanks, Tony."

Back at the table Janine seemed to fancy me, and in spite of Sammy's frantic efforts she didn't want to know. She asked me to dance, and tossed the sad starlet's mane of red hair, and wriggled the sad starlet's curvy body, and the accent twanged.

We ended up in my flat. I just don't like going home alone.

I was loaded, and she didn't stop talking. I heard all about the movie she was doing, some bit part in a B film, no doubt, and how Franklin was very sweet but such a baby, and how she loved London, and how Hobo was such a great place and, just as I got it in, she said, "Can I have a free membership?" So I gave it to her.

That's life.

# 7

## ALEXANDRA

What a week! It has rushed by, and so much has happened. Maddy and I have our own apartment in Chelsea, and on Monday I start a job, and tonight I've got a date with Michael.

He telephoned yesterday and said that he and a friend of his were going to take us out. Maddy answered the phone and I was trying to listen. "Do you want to go?" she whispered to me.

"Yes," I whispered back, "of course I do." So it was settled, much to my delight, and they were picking us up at eight.

Maddy and I discussed the Peter Lincoln Smith incident and we both came to the conclusion that he behaved like an idiot.

I have secretly decided that Michael and I should have an affair. Maddy and I talked about birth control for hours. Maddy says we should find a nice old doctor to prescribe the pill for us. It certainly sounds a lot easier than all the other undignified methods. I mean they all seem so *complicated*.

Between us our sexual experience is very limited. I have been kissed by three boys, including Peter, and Maddy about the same, although, of course, she had been sort of semi-stripped when the school gardener got her bra and sweater off. Maddy said she felt all sort of weak-kneed when he had kissed her there and sucked on her nipples like a baby. But then he had been angry when she wouldn't let him go any farther.

Maddy has small breasts. Mine are bigger. I feel all embarrassed when I think of Michael looking at them.

"I wonder what Jonathan Roberts is like," Madelaine suddenly said. "Isn't it funny that Michael wants to be your date. Maybe I'll have you as a sister-in-law!" She giggled.

I blushed. "Don't be so silly. He's just being nice to us because we don't know anyone in London."

"Huh! Michael's never been nice to me before. In fact, he's very selfish. *I* think he's after your body, your pure white virgin body."

Michael and his friend Jonathan were a half-hour late. I felt sure they had forgotten all about us.

Jonathan seemed quite nice, and Madelaine looked pleased.

Michael said, "Well girls, we're going to show you the town." He looked terrific in a yellow roll-neck sweater and black trousers.

We all piled into Jonathan's Mini, Maddy and me in the back. They took us to a very small cellar restaurant, absolutely jammed with people, and we sat at a corner table, scrubbed pine with a black candle in a glass holder. Very romantic, but rather noisy.

I was sitting opposite Michael and he leaned across and said, "You don't look too bad tonight, London suits you."

Oh, what a wonderful evening!

We drank red wine and ate chicken casserole. Madelaine got on well with Jonathan, and Michael was really nice to me. In fact, the best thing was when he said to me at the end of the meal. "You know for a girl you're quite intelligent."

It was past twelve when we left, and Michael held my hand.

"What shall we do now?" Jonathan said to Michael. "Want to pop into Judie's for some dancing?"

"Can't stand that place, it's always filled with such a grim crew."

'How about Hobo?' I ventured It hadn't been much fun for me before but with Michael it would be different.

'I'm not a member," he said. 'and they're very sticky about letting non-members in."

"That's all right," I said, "my father sort of has money in the place. We'll get in.'

"Not on a Saturday night," Jonathan said 'Hobo's the hottest place in town."

"I'm *sure* it will be all right." I felt rather proud of the fact that they all seemed to think the place was so exclusive. I tried to remember the name of the manager. Tony something–Beard, Bird—I wasn't quite sure.

"Look, if Alex says it's O.K., let's go." Madelaine said.

"It will be a wasted trip," Jonathan replied, "that place is impossible. You've got to be Marlon Brando at least."

"Come on, Marlon," Michael said with a grin, squeezing my hand. "Show us the impossible!"

I hoped I could.

# 8

# TONY

A week has passed. I saw four movies, had dinner at Trader Vic's, lost twenty-five pounds at roulette, bought three new shirts, and got laid every night.

Fontaine has gone, taken off on one of her trips. She never tells me she's going, just buzzes off. I suppose she thinks it's good to keep me in suspense.

Janine has sort of moved herself in and I can't seem to get rid of her. "The Twang," as I call her, seems to think she's here to stay. She comes to the club every night and sits with the gang, and then she comes home with me and rushes off to the studio a few hours later. She's back at seven—just about when I'm getting up.

She's not a bad bird after all, very accommodating. But she'll have to go. I haven't even had a chance to call Sadie this week.

It's Saturday, big bright Saturday, busiest night of the week. It's eight P.M. and I'm seriously thinking of getting up. "The Twang" is still asleep. Well, I mean she's knocking herself out, poor little bird. Not so little—she's built like a brick shithouse.

I need a new apartment. This pad I have is very small. When Fontaine gets back, we're going to have a serious talk about money. I need more, I deserve more. Every night except Sunday from ten P.M. till four A.M. is no joke.

I think I shall wear the black silk turtleneck and new black slacks tonight. That's where all my bread goes—on gear. Well, I have to look smart, keep up an image. It's important in my business. No use looking like one of those long hairs—dirty and all that. I reckon I've got a good look and I'm going to stick with it.

I mean I don't have short hair—not by any means. It sort of curls around the back of my collar—just right. If I'm lucky I can get out of here before "The Twang" wakes up.

I wasn't lucky. She caught me at the door. "Babee," she squealed, "wait for me, where are we going?"

Oh, shit! That meant she expected me to buy her dinner.

I waited while she wriggled her starlet's body into a too-tight white dress and teased her hair and put on her eyelashes. She was definitely becoming a drag.

I called Sammy. He had a date, so we joined up with him at a little Italian bistro and dined royally on spaghetti and meatballs.

Sammy's date was fifteen if she was a day. He had picked her up at a bus stop. One of Sammy's habits was to cruise the streets in his secondhand E-type Jag looking for likely birds. He never copped out, always came up with something. I guess they liked secondhand E-types. One of his favorite stories was of how he followed a bus from Baker Street to the Elephant and Castle because he fancied some little darling on it and, according to him, he made it at the end of the ride! One of these days he was going to get himself in a lot of trouble. Some tough father was going to ram his fist down his throat. Anyway, until that day came, he was happy.

After dinner we went to the club. I liked to get there early on Saturday. It was too soon for anyone to be in. Flowers was playing a few far-out sounds. Franco was screaming in Italian at his waiters, Tina was polishing her nails.

"The Twang" and the fifteen-year-old went off to the ladies' room where they stayed at least a half-hour.

"What do birds do to their faces that takes so long?" Sammy said.

" 'Ere, what's with you and this American bit, going a bit strong, isn't it?"

"Sammy, Sammy, you know me better than that. As a matter of fact I wondered if you wouldn't mind stepping in."

Sammy shook his head sadly. "She had her chance. Anyway, she's a bit old for me."

Janine was all of twenty-five.

To tell the truth, I felt rather bad about Franklin. I knew he was choked up about her latching onto me. I wish I could talk her into showing him the ropes—in other words, get him in the sack with her. He was a great-looking kid, some lucky girl was in for a thrill. I mean he'd been saving it up for a long time!

They started to come in. As usual, the ones who weren't too sure of a good table came first. It always reminded me of a show. The audience files quietly in, sits down and waits, then come the performers. Yelling greetings, kissing everyone, wearing maxi, mini, caftans, flowers, bells—you name it, they wear it. The beautiful people. An assorted group of high-frequency talent, and every one of them my friend.

On Saturday you get the one-night-out-a-week group, too. Dressed to kill, they make a lot of uncool noise. However, they have the bread and run up the really big bills, so you have to put up with them.

Here comes a group of them now. Hymie Verne Blatt, dress manufacturer, and his heavily bejeweled wife Ethel Verne Blatt, with Jack Davidsonly, coat manufacturer, and his even more heavily bejeweled wife Bessie Davidsonly. What a group! Every time the wives went out of town, which was often, Hymie and Jack would appear with a pair of ding-a-lings—proud as punch. Meanwhile, from what I heard, Ethel and Bessie were making it with a couple of Spanish beach boys in Majorca!

However, tonight they were all a happy family. Neither couple had ever been known to appear anywhere alone; there were always the four of them, or the two guys, or the two wives. Did they fuck together? We all wondered.

What a greeting I got when I went over to their table! You would think I was their closest, dearest friend. These were the same four people who wouldn't look at me sideways when I was a waiter—many's the time I'd Caesared their salad.

"Who's coming in tonight, Tony doll?" Ethel asked anxiously. She was the blond one. Bessie was dark. They obviously thought they were a hot team together, appealing to all types.

I gave her a kiss on the cheek, standard procedure. "You'll see, you'll see." I had four types of greeting routine. Big stars I didn't know, a firm handshake, sexy look. Big stars I did know, kiss-kiss. Ding-a-lings and swingers (female or male), hug and a kiss. Everyone else a kiss on the cheek.

The evening was starting to swing. It was going to be a good one. On a Saturday night we could do with a hundred more tables and fill them all. Who would have thought that people would fight and struggle to get into a hot, smoky, crowded atmosphere with deafening music? But they did and they loved it.

Franklin arrived girlless and sad-faced. He sat and stared at "The Twang."

Hal arrived with an American widow to whom he was showing the sights of London. What an operator! Always dressed to kill in the best Savile Row had to offer, handmade shoes, Turnbull and Asser shirts, and a lot of gold from his fillings to his cufflinks. Meanwhile he was flat on the heels of his ass, busted, broke. His last fifty pounds had gone to the kid brother in New Jersey.

He lived in the best hotels, promoting here, promoting there, and there was always some rich old bag to bail him out. This one tonight was a real horror. From the blue-rinsed hair to the sagging body. Oh, boy, Hal certainly had to work somewhere along the line, and I didn't envy him.

Franco was patting me on the shoulder, we were reaching jamming up point, and there were only a few emergency tables left. Someone at reception was asking for me. Shit! He knew I never went out front on Saturday night. Too embarrassing turning people away. He muttered something about friends of Benjamin Khaled's. Well, they could go screw. No room, not on a Saturday, baby. On second thought, maybe I should give them the bad news myself. People never said they were friends of Benjamin's, it was always "Fontaine insisted we come by," and then they were shocked when they got a bill.

I went out front. There were two young guys, a sandy-haired girl and another one talking to Tina.

"I'm sorry," I said, "but we just don't have a table—you know it's . . ."

The girl talking to Tina turned around.

My stomach did a somersault. It was Alexandra. She gazed at me with big brown eyes and smiled tentatively. She had a gorgeous smile.

"Hello, do you remember me?" she said softly.

Did I remember her—ha!

"Of course I do." What should I call her? Alexandra? Miss? Alexandra Khaled?

She said, "Couldn't you just squeeze us in somewhere? Daddy said it would be all right."

As if I would turn her away, even without the threat of "Daddy." She looked different, prettier. Her auburn hair was loose, kept off her face with a green headband, and she wore a matching green sweater and tweedy slacks. Nothing flashy, but she looked great.

"I'm sure we'll find room for you. How many? Four?"

She nodded, well pleased, and attached herself to the arm of one of the fellows. I felt an immediate dislike for him.

It was then I had a flash of inspiration and decided to jam them all onto my table. What a great idea!

I led them in and told Sammy, etc., to move over. They all looked annoyed. The table was crowded as it was. But I managed to get the four of them seated. Then I offered them a drink and was shocked when Alexandra agreed to have wine with the other three. I had sort of imagined that she didn't drink.

They chatted among themselves while I hovered by the table. Sammy pantomimed a face at me as much as to say—what the hell is this?

I really don't know why I flipped for this girl, but I had, and this time I wasn't going to let her get away.

I studied the schmuck she was with. Casually dressed, slightly long hair, much too good-looking in a boyish way. He had an arm around her and was tapping her shoulder in time to the music. This was certainly no creepy little Peter Lincoln Smith. This was probably the boy friend. Well, we would soon find out.

"The Twang" suddenly yelled at me across the table, "Can we dance, sweetie?"

I froze her with a grim look. Stupid loudmouth! Got to get rid of her. "Franklin, dance with Janine," I said pleasantly. Silently I said—for Christ's sake give her a grope and get her interested in you.

They went off to dance. Well, that was a start. I sat down. I stuck out my hand to Alexandra's boy friend, forcing him to take his arm from around her. "Tony Blake, glad to see you."

Alexandra said, "Oh, I'm sorry—this is Michael Newcombe." Then she indicated the other two, "Michael's sister Madelaine, and Jonathan Roberts."

We all shook hands.

"Super of you to squeeze us in," Madelaine said. "We didn't believe Alex when she said she could get us in. Michael's been trying to come here for ages!"

That made Michael out to be a right idiot.

"I hope you like it," I said. "Saturday night's a real killer."

Sammy leaned over, his cockney accent cutting the air, " 'Ere—take a look at that."

We all turned to see Massey and Suki come in. She was wearing the shortest dress ever, split under the arms to below the waist at the side. It was a good job she was flat chested. Even then, it was some dress. What with her huge made-up clown face, her mannish haircut and white face, she looked like she was in drag.

Massey was cool as ever. "Hey man."

They squashed down at the table and I could see Michael giving Suki a stare. Good. I performed the introductions and soon everyone was talking.

Alexandra had one of those classless, beautiful speaking voices. She really was a knockout, and she was nice. She wasn't a stupid little rich bitch as I had thought. Her friends, of course, were a bit on the square side, hadn't been around much, I reckoned. From the conversation I gathered that Madelaine and Alexandra had been at a finishing school together in Switzerland.

Michael hadn't taken his eyes off Suki, and I could see Alexandra getting a bit edgy. What an idiot he was to stare at a freak like Suki with a girl like Alexandra by his side. Still it was just as well, what did he know, he was your typical well-educated-student type. I willed him to ask sweet little Suki to dance. Sweet little Suki indeed. She was the typical model, all legs and no tits. Massey and she had been going together for a few months on and off, and though they both appeared regularly with other dates, they had a nice scene going.

Bingo. Michael the jerk was asking her to dance. I thought for a second the dumb face was going to refuse, but no, she couldn't resist the opportunity of wriggling her backside. She got up. Michael got up. Alexandra frowned.

Madelaine looked embarrassed and started to chatter loudly. I grabbed my opportunity like a sinking diver. "Come and take a look around the club," I said directly to Alexandra.

"Super," Madelaine replied.

Alexandra shook her head. "I think I'll stay here."

I glared at Madelaine who had gotten up, and then to cap it all Jonathan asked Alexandra to dance and off they went.

Have you ever been choked!

I caught Franco's eye, then said to Madelaine, "We'll have to take a rain check, I'm wanted out front."

Tina was patiently turning people away. She smiled at me. She looked tired and pale. I guess it was no joke living with Flowers—he probably never quieted down. "How's it going?" I gave her a pat.

"Fine, Mr. Blake." She brushed a lock of blond hair off her forehead.

I felt sorry for her. "Go home early tonight, you look tired—I'll get Franco to bring one of the boys out front."

"Oh, thank you. I don't feel too good . . ."

I went back inside and hovered by the dance floor. Alexandra was making an attempt to shake. She wasn't very good at it. I studied her body partly visible through the folds of clothes. A nice full bosom, slim waist, small hips and long legs. Was she or wasn't she? Did she or didn't she? I had a hard-on to find out.

Madelaine was dancing. Sammy and his teenage wonder were nowhere to be seen. Franklin and "The Twang" were sitting down.

"Hi, Tony," a girl I knew said on her way back from dancing. She was very pretty. She squeezed my arm, "When am I going to see you?"

I honestly couldn't remember if we'd made it or not. Some nights I was so loaded I wouldn't have known who it was wriggling about underneath me.

She was with a well-known singer, Steve Scott. One of the new breed, trying to project the sexy Englishman image and not doing a bad job. She was a dancer, a swinger, I did remember her. Her name was Carolyn something or other. I went over and sat with them and bought them a drink.

"Want to come to a party tomorrow?" Steve

asked. "My place, all you need is a bottle and a bird."

"Yeah," I was half catching glimpses of Alexandra dancing through the throng.

"You must come, it will be great," Carolyn said. She jotted down Steve's address, which I absentmindedly stuck in my pocket. Who needed parties on a Sunday anyway?

Flowers was launching into some slow soul sounds, and when I glimpsed Alexandra again, she was clutched in the schmuck she was dancing with's arms. Well, Flowers could forget that. I rushed over to him and made him change mid-record to something fast. Automatically, Alexandra and partner jerked apart. I noticed happily that Suki and Michael didn't.

Massey noticed too. "Think I've lost her," he joked when I sat down, "always knew she'd go off with the first white cat that came on strong."

Now—how about Massey and "The Twang"? No—she didn't like spades unless they were stars, and he didn't like busty chicks. Oh, well . . .

Alexandra was coming back to the table. She looked flushed. "It looks like we've been deserted, Jonathan," she said with a wry grin to schmucko. I took her arm, which she politely but immediately pulled away.

Oh, God, her skin felt like velvet.

"Listen, I want to make you (should I add

the rest of the sentence?) a member. Let's go to the office."

"Now?" she looked surprised. "It's very nice of you, but I don't think . . ."

I didn't let her finish. "You've got to be a member, it will only take a minute, and then you can come here anytime without having to go through the whole bit."

"O.K." she got up. "Come on, Jonathan."

He got up too, and thinking fast I said, "You stay here, otherwise the table will jam up and there will be nowhere for you to sit when we get back."

He sat down. I had her.

This time I took a firm grip on her arm and propelled her through the crush. She was looking over the dance floor to see Michael and Suki. I got her out to reception and then down one flight of stairs to the office. It was quite dark and only the faintest sounds of music reached us. I unlocked the door and switched on the light. It was a bare room with filing cabinets, a desk, and a couple of chairs, very unromatic.

She stretched and yawned, her breasts taut against her sweater.

I had the mad urge to grab her, strip off her clothes, and make violent love to her. This little bird had really got under my skin. But it would never do to rush things. To get her out of my system I had to have her. and to have her I had to play it cool

I lit a cigarette and she sat down, tapped impatient buff nails on the desk, and said, "Who's that awful girl Michael's dancing with?"

I sang a few off-key lines of an old song. "Jealousy."

She glared at me. "I'm not jealous, I can assure you," she stuck her chin out, a gesture I immediately loved. "But she's just ghastly Who is she?"

"Some dopey model. Is Michael your boy friend?"

"Oh, no," she flushed. "Actually, we've known each other ages, he being Madelaine's brother and everything, but this is the first time we've been out together"

The scene became clear: schoolgirl crush, the fancied-him-since-she-was-a-little-girl bit. Well, we would soon get rid of him.

I found a membership form and doodled on it with a chewed pencil that was on the desk. She looked at me expectantly, wide brown eyes, beautiful eyes.

"What's your address?" I asked. She made me nervous.

"I wonder if I should give you my mother's address," she mused aloud. "I shall probably be there every weekend and it is my proper address."

I didn't want her mother's address, I wanted her improper address

She licked her lips, they were very full and shiny and with some kind of lip gloss, very sexy. "No, perhaps I should give you my address here, although I don't know how permanent it will be"

Was she a virgin? No, impossible. There was no virgins left over the age of fourteen in London. Even Sammy hasn't come across one yet.

"Madelaine and I are sharing a flat," she said, rather proudly. "Can Madelaine be a member too? The address is 14 Dundee Court. Chelsea."

Chelsea yet! What did she want to go and set herself up in the middle of all that mob for? Oh, well, at least she was in London and not living with either Mummy or Daddy. "Phone number?" I asked, silently rehearsing what I would say the first time I called.

She gave me the number and I said, "That's great, we'll send you the card this week, and then I expect to see lots of you."

She blushed. There were actually girls that still know how to blush.

"I doubt it," she said standing up. "I start my job on Monday, and I have to be there by nine every day."

"Nine in the morning?" My voice was incredulous. Nine in the morning was ridiculous.

She smiled, "That's right, I'm a secretary."

Was I going mad, or was there a definite note of pride in her voice?

A secretary indeed! Could this possibly be Benjamin Khaled's daughter? I was choked, but so what, I still fancied her even if she didn't have any money. The old bastard, making her work. Fontaine was clad from head to toe in mink, and this poor little bird had to go out to work. What a game.

Still it was just as well. If she'd had money everyone would have thought I was after that.

She was at the door, anxious to get back to see what Michael was up to, no doubt. I stayed sitting at the desk like an idiot.

"Shall we go back?" she said politely.

Didn't she realize I fancied her? Couldn't she tell? She treated me like I was nobody special. I mean, I don't want to sound big-headed, but I do run the place, and everybody likes me. And I do have a good look, and she should bloody well pay me some attention. Running after some little long-haired student, the girl was mad.

We went upstairs and Tina gave me a knowing smile.

At the table Sammy said, loud voiced as ever. " 'Ere, where you been?" And then "The Twang" had the nerve to say "Tony, babee, you're neglecting me. Let's dance."

That was the end of her. She had gone far

enough. She could pack her false eyelashes and hank of hair and go.

Alexandra said a trifle irritably, "Is Michael still dancing?"

Madelaine nodded and looked embarrassed. I seized the opportunity and, grabbing Alexandra before she could sit down, said, "If you can't beat 'em, join 'em." And I whipped her off to the dance floor.

I vaguely heard "The Twang" shrieking in astonishment, "Son of a bitch!"

Alexandra let me hold her at a discreet arm's length to the beat of "Jimmy Mack." I signaled Flowers to put on some slow sounds, and she said, "You girl friend's furious."

"My girl friend?" I looked amazed. "I've never seen her before tonight."

She smiled, that insane innocent smile, and I pulled her a little closer as Flowers switched to "Groovin'." She struggled a bit, but I had her in a tight grip and I wasn't letting go. She smelled of clean hair and toothpaste. I could feel her full breasts against me and her narrow waist was firm against my hands. She felt every bit as good as I'd expected her to.

"Isn't that Steven Scott?" she asked suddenly. He and Carolyn were wrapped casually around each other close by.

"Yeah—why? You like him?"

"Oh, yes," she was like a little schoolgirl, "I

always buy his records, I think he's a terrific singer."

Any second I expected her to produce an autograph book. She was a real sweet innocent.

Suddenly I had a great idea, "I'll tell you what I'll do for you since you're so nice."

She looked at me with those big brown eyes.

"How would you like to go to a party at Steve Scott's house tomorrow?"

"Really? You mean I'd actually meet him?"

"Sure, I'll take you. How's that?"

She pondered a bit. "Have you been invited?"

Oh, this girl was too much! I nodded seriously. "Of course. We'll go, O.K.?"

"Can Madelaine come?"

Fuck bloody Madelaine, I was getting good and fed up with her. "That might be a bit tricky, but we'll go anyway."

She made a snap decision. "All right, but I can't stay out late."

Had I made a wise move? Steve's parties were always a bit of an orgy. Well, that was O.K. We could always leave and go somewhere else—a nice romantic little restaurant, or my place, my sumptuous gaff off the Edgware Road. I kept on meaning to move, but who had had the bread?

Flowers gave me a freaky look as we danced by. "Man, who is the disc jockey tonight?" he muttered, rolling mad eyeballs. Sometimes he got very tempermental. He would go on kicks of playing far-out sounds that nobody knew and then when he was told to play something a little more popular he would sulk for days. At other times he was so stoned he didn't even know what he was playing. But when he was good, forget it. He could make the room move like nobody else. He was great.

Alexandra said, "What shall I wear?"

All birds are forever asking that question and you know they already have the whole outfit planned.

"Nothing dressy, whatever you fancy."

Perhaps she would fancy something with a long back zip that I could get her out of in next to no time.

I must say I had been neglecting the club since Alexandra had arrived, but it suddenly came to my notice that a great struggle was going on in the corner, and all I could see was the backs of three waiters and a worried looking Franco. Alexandra felt so good I didn't want to let her go, but there was always tomorrow. Business was business. I gave her a gentle push in the direction of our table, "Be a good girl and go sit down. I sense a little trouble."

Steward Wade, a drunken bum actor, was sitting on the floor screaming four-letter words at the waiters while they answered back angrily in Italian. They were trying to pick him up and he was landing a drunken punch anywhere he could.

"What's the trouble?" I asked Franco.

He waved his arms around excitedly. "The punk, 'ee no wanna pay 'ees bill. 'Ee broke one of my boys' noses, 'ee say 'ee never pay bill anywhere."

I pushed through the waiters.

"Come on, Stew baby," I said, "let's not cause a scene. On your feet."

"Ah, Tony," he had one of those booming Shakespearean voices. "Tell your frigging waiters to leave me the fuck alone."

"Come on, sweetheart, let's go and talk about it outside."

"I want to stay here." He sat there, all two hundred pounds of him, with a childish drunken smile. "Fuck the lot of you," he shouted gleefully. "I'm Steward Wade, *the* Steward Wade. I never pay, so fuck you."

The waiters were muttering angrily among themselves.

"Pick him up and throw him out," I said. I'd had enough. Customers like him we didn't need.

Happy in their work, the four waiters grabbed him by the legs and arms and proceeded to carry him out bodily while he bellowed "I'll get the frigging police." Then he passed out cold. A large scrubber in a micro mini with legs like a football player scurried out after him.

Franco and I looked at each other and shrugged. You get used to anything in our business.

Back at our table Michael and Suki had finally returned, and Alexandra was saying she wanted to go. So were Madelaine and Jonathan, but Michael was saying nothing, just looking a bit glassy-eyed in Suki's direction as she studied her face in a Mary Quant make-up box.

"I say, could we get the bill" Jonathan asked.

"That's all right." I looked at Alexandra who was looking at Michael. "It's on me."

"Oh, that's awfully nice of you," Madelaine said. She wasn't bad in a debby sort of way. A suitable roommate for Alexandra, not flighty, a bit homely.

They all got up and exchanged good-byes around the table. I walked them out front. I managed to pull Alexandra to the side, "I'll pick you up around eight tomorrow."

"Oh fine," she looked like she had forgotten all about it.

They piled into the elevator and left. The last glimpse I got of her she was staring accusingly at Michael. She opened her mouth to say something, but the elevator doors closed.

I stretched in anticipation of the following night. I would soon have her forgetting all about Michael.

It was two A.M. peak time. Flowers came strolling out, the group had just gone on. "Just going around the corner, man," he said. Off to get high, he at least had enough sense not to smoke in the club.

Hal appeared with his blue-rinsed lady friend. I had to admire him, he certainly had a lot of style. "We're going to play a little chemmy," he announced, giving me the wink. That meant he was going to play a little chemin de fer with *her* money. He was a mad gambler and sometimes won a bundle which he would immediately blow on new gear.

She smiled at me, rows of nicotine-stained teeth, "I just love you little old club, honey."

Hal said, "Mamie's got a girl friend coming in next week, if you want to make up a foursome."

A girl friend yet! She was about sixty! I shook my head seriously, "I'm engaged."

"Oh, what a shame, honey, she would have loved you."

He was a bum. He knew I didn't go for the rich old widow scene, yet he never gave up, he was always trying to recruit me.

"You and I as a team, Tony, we'd destroy them," he would say.

Fontaine was enough for me, thank you. I could just about make it with her, although it was becoming more and more difficult.

Fontaine—I had forgotten about her, what with her being away and all. But I glumly supposed she would be back soon. How would she feel about me and Alexandra? I pondered this fact and decided she wouldn't like it at all. It was a tricky situation. If I had any sense I wouldn't go near Miss Alexandra Khaled with a ten-foot pole.

But I had flipped for her, she had really knocked me out. So let's face it, I wasn't playing it too smart, but so what, Fontaine would never find out, and Alexandra and I could have a fast affair then bye-bye. "Schmuck," a little voice kept saying in my ear, but I ignored it.

"Well, baby, I guess you and I can call it quits," a furious voice said. It was "The Twang," all quivering, sexy five-foot-five of her.

I wanted to say, "Yes, you're right," but Alexandra had put me in the mood, and "The Twang" was there and ready, and there didn't seem to be much else available stock around. One more night with her wouldn't be too much of a hardship. I patted her sexy ass. "Customers, my lovely. I've got to be nice to the paying people." She pouted, and I put my arm around her, "Let's dance."

# 9

# FONTAINE

New York is cold. The people in the streets and shops are boring. They all seem to discover you're English and to them this means instant friendship; they think they can chat with you for hours about their dreary grandma in Scunthorpe. Today a perfect stranger came up to me in Bendel's, and demanded in a deep Southern drawl where had I got my chinchilla. Why, she practically ripped it off my back with her eyes. However, they are chic, the very rich women.

Ray has become the darling of the society set. They all pop in to him for their comb-outs. Actually, he's become a bit effeminate, I'm shocked! He who was always so virile. Maybe it's my imagination, but I'm not usually wrong about these things. He hasn't even approached me about going to bed together. Success has definitely gone to his head.

After a week here I find myself thinking about Tony. A week of nothing sexually, only a short two-hour affair with the husband of a friend of mine. Nothing special, rather boring actually.

It would be rather amusing to have Tony here for a few days. Show the sexy animal off. I could tell Benjamin I wanted him to see New York, to find out what he thinks about opening a Hobo here. Tony would love it. I could buy him some clothes, show him the city.

Yes, I shall call Benjamin tonight and have him arrange the whole thing. Tony could be here by Monday and we can fly back together the following weekend.

I dressed carefully. Lunch at 21 with Sarah, wife of the man I'd had the two-hour affair with. I knew she wanted to tell me about her latest lover. The gossip around town said he was a Chinese waiter. Well Sarah has always been kinky, so I wasn't surprised.

Sarah would adore Tony. She's a very well-educated society matron in her thirties, thin and beautiful; we used to model together. She married a Texas oil millionaire, then a California real estate millionaire, and now Alan, attractive unsuccessful writer. She has loads of money and Alan spends it well. They both have affairs and neither seems to mind. Actually she would be rather pleased if I told her about Alan and me. He wasn't very good though, a disappointment. All artistic merit and no balls!

Sarah looked divine. If ever I decided to turn lesbian, she would be my choice. Thin Slavic face, jet black hair dramatically plastered down with a center part. She wore yellow, this year's Dior; I was a little more avant garde in Yves Saint Laurent.

We started with champagne cocktails and ordered melon and steak. Life is a permanent diet.

"Tell me all," I demanded.

She smiled dreamily. "Fontaine, my darling, if you haven't tried the mysteries of the East you haven't lived."

I smiled back, "I like my men a little, shall we say taller?"

She giggled. "It's the quality not the quantity."

"Give me quantity, to hell with quality!"

It was a pleasant lunch, I always enjoyed being with Sarah. We are alike in many ways.

Later I called Benjamin. "Darling, I've got a marvelous idea. What about a Hobo here? Yes, here in New York. Can you arrange to have Tony sent over for a few days? Now, immediately, tomorrow if possible. You're wonderful. Of course I miss you. Yes, darling, have your secretary call me back with the details. Yes, of course I'll be home soon. I love you too. Bye." Poor old Benjamin.

Oh, well, a party at the Sidwell's tonight. Better dazzle them with the new Courrèges. Soon I would be dazzling them all with Tony. What fun!

# 10

## ALEXANDRA

Madelaine and I sat up late on Saturday talking when we got back from Hobo. I have decided I'm in love with Michael!

I was forced to tell her how I felt because I simply had to tell someone, and since she was his sister and my best friend, perhaps she could help.

She roared with laughter when she heard. "Sloppy old Michael! You're joking, I hope." But then she could see that I wasn't, and she got very serious and said, "Alex, he's terrible with girls. He just wants them for one thing and then drops them."

I didn't see how Maddy could know that. After all she had been away at school with me for most of the year. Anyway, if he wanted that one thing from me, he could have it. Although I was furious about him chatting up that awful model girl all night.

"Look how jealous you are," Maddy said. "The thing is we have got to make him jealous of you. I think he quite likes you, only I don't think he looks on you as a potential girl friend. After all, you've known each other since we were all kids together."

"He still thinks I am a kid," I said miserably, "he said so."

"We've just got to make him realize how super and desirable you are." Maddy's eyes were gleaming, she loved organizing things. "Tomorrow night, when Tony thingy comes to fetch us—oh, I do hope I can come, too—well, we'll get Michael to be here, and you'll sweep past him looking absolutely gorgeous, and sort of act very cold and offhand with him."

"Do you really think I should go to Steve Scott's party with Tony? And anyway how do I look absolutely gorgeous? I haven't got anything to wear."

We went through my wardrobe and the only thing remotely glamorous I possessed was a frilly dressing gown.

"You can wear that!" Maddy exclaimed. "It's super. Put a belt around it and no one will know."

I tried it on, and with shoes and a belt it really did look quite good. So I decided I would wear that and we finally got to bed at three A.M. I was exhausted.

Maddy phoned Michael the next morning. Actually it was about twelve o'clock as we both overslept.

'We're in frightful trouble." she wailed. 'We've blown a fuse and I can't work the television, and the stopper's jammed in the bath."

'Christ!" Michael complained. I was listening on the extension "All right. I'll come over when I get up."

'We've got to go out now. Do you think you could make it about seven?"

'Seven! Where the bloody hell are you going?"

'We have to go and see Alex's father. Is seven O.K. then?"

'Yes. I suppose so, but I can't take you for dinner if that's what you're getting at. I've got a date."

'That's O.K.," Maddy said sweetly, and hung up, giggling. "All fixed." she declared. "Now you've got to really devastate him."

We spent the afternoon in preparation.

When Michael arrived I was shut in the bedroom with my hair in rollers trying to do a decent make-up job. My hand shook and I smudged the eyeliner. so I had to take it all off and start again.

Maddy was ready. She had promised to keep Michael busy until Tony arrived. I wasn't supposed to come out of the bedroom until Tony got there, then I was supposed to just glide out and practically ignore Michael.

I was only just ready by eight. I heard the doorbell.

Oh, well, here goes.

# 11

# TONY

It's four o'clock in the afternoon and there's no getting rid of "The Twang." It's her day of rest and she's making the most of it. Fast asleep like a lump of clay, unmade-up face hidden beneath a tangle of hair. In the daylight it's orange and quite revolting; she says its photographs fantastically. She's very ambitious. I'm also ambitious—ambitious to get her out of my bed and on her way.

I gave her a gentle tap on the shoulder. She snuggled down in the bed and snored softly. Oh, man, the only thing that was going to wake her was something I didn't feel like giving her this morning.

I went in the bathroom and washed. She

slept on. I made coffee and turned the telly up loud. She didn't stir. I gave her a shove. She sighed and stretched out tarantula arms. I ignored them. She opened sleep-filled eyes and said, "C'mon back to bed, baby."

Really, she and Sammy would have been great together.

"Get up, Janine," I said. "My mother's coming to visit."

"Your mother?" Her eyes snapped wide open and she sat up revealing full orange-tipped boobs fresh out of the center spread in *Playboy*.

"Yeah, my mother. She takes it into her head once a year to come. Today's the day."

"Oh, shit," Janine twanged, and got up.

She was built, although without makeup her face was puffy and washed out. It's amazing what makeup can do for a girl.

She stomped into the bathroom and closed the door. I congratulated myself on the mother bit, and tidied up. I could go out, get something to eat, and then get ready to pick up Alexandra. I wanted the pad to be in good shape in case she wished to view it.

Janine emerged an hour later, face in place, figure in sweater and too short skirt. Her kind of figure just didn't go with mini-mini's.

She was playing it cool trying to look like she didn't care too much. I had gathered her things together in case she hadn't gotten the hint.

She smiled at me coolly. "Bye, sweetheart," she said. "See you around." Exit. "The Twang."

I phoned Sammy.

"Oh, what a night," he moaned. "The little raver wouldn't leave me alone."

"You want to grab something to eat?" I asked him.

"Yeah, pick me up."

I pulled on old gear and drove over to his place, five minutes away, I was driving some decrepit old Mini that a girl friend had left with me to look after while she did a dancing tour of the Far East. I wondered if Sammy could be conned into lending me his E-type for tonight. Very sexy, this E-type, a low slung, roaring phallic symbol.

Sammy looked terrible, still in his dressing gown, unshaven and seedy eyed. "I'm giving up the young ones," he announced. "Too much bloody energy."

We went to a salt beef hangout nearby, and I listened to the tale of Miss Fifteen-year-old's sexy acrobatics.

"And to top it all," Sammy concluded, "she pinched a fiver from beside the bed when she left. Liberty!"

By this time it was half past six and I wanted to get home and changed for Alexandra. "What are you doing tonight, Samuel?" I asked.

"Going to bed, I'm knocked out."

"Can I borrow your car?"

"What for? You've got the Mini."

"Oh, come on, Sammy. I've got an important date. I can't take her in that."

"Who is it?" Sammy was like a nosy old woman.

I kept my voice casual. "You know, the bird from last night, Alexandra."

"She's not your style," Sammy said in surprise. "You like flashier models than that."

"I like her," I said shortly. "Can I borrow it?"

"Sure, only I've got to 'ave it by eight tomorrow morning."

He tossed me the keys and I gave him the keys to the Mini. He was all right Sammy was.

At home the phone was ringing and under my door was a telegram. I picked up the receiver and flipped open the buff-colored envelope.

"Mr. Blake?" a crisp, efficient feminine voice said. "This is Alice, Mr. Khaled's secretary. I've been trying to get you all day, but your line's been out of order."

I always take the phone off the hook when I'm asleep.

"Yeah," I said. Maybe Fontaine had had an accident.

"Mr. Khaled requires that you fly to New York to investigate the suitability of opening a Hobo there."

"What?" I was stunned.

"Mrs. Khaled suggests you leave immediately. I actually had you booked on the eight P.M. flight, but I shouldn't think you'll make that now. Of course if you rushed . . ."

I interrupted. "I can't go tonight, a death in the family, you know." I always have been an exaggerated liar.

"Oh," the crisp voice paused. "Well, how about seven forty-five tomorrow morning?"

What the hell was this? What was all the urgency? Of course I would love to see New York, but what was with the panic? I scanned the wire quickly.

NEED YOU HERE STOP BENJAMIN WILL EXPLAIN STOP MAKE IT FAST. FONTAINE.

"How long am I supposed to go for?" I asked Alice.

"A few days, I believe. Is the seven forty-five all right?"

"Yes, that's O.K."

"Fine. A car will pick you up at six A.M., everything will be taken care of at this end, a car will meet you on arrival. Bon Voyage!" Alice's crisp voice hung up.

I sat there. What about visas and everything? I thought it took months. What should I take? Hobo in New York. What a scene *that* would be!

There was no time to waste. I didn't want to

be late for Alexandra. I'm off to New York in the morning—sounded good.

I sorted out some things to take, counted my money, only twenty quid. Well, I supposed Fontaine would take care of that. Then I dressed. Best casual clobber. Groomed the barnet. I was ready.

Alexandra and Madelaine lived in a big, grim block of flats. I rang the bell of No. 14 and waited. I was shocked when Madelaine's brother Michael answered. He was unconcerned at seeing me, and invited me into an old-fashioned large living room. Madelaine bounced in next, dressed in a flouncy blue dress, and said, "Is it going to be all right for me to come too?"

I looked sad. "Sorry darling, absolutely not. I warned Alex."

"Oh," Madelaine's bounce sagged a bit, but she lit a cigarette and coughed. Then she brightened. "Well, Alex can tell me all about it, anyway." She wasn't a bad little bird, certainly understanding.

Michael offered me a drink. He acted like he lived there. Then, enter Alexandra. She looked lovely in one of those Victorian dresses with frills everywhere; her hair was tied back and she looked really young and pretty. I was knocked out.

Michael said, "You've got everything but the kitchen stove on."

She glared at him and replied, "Better than wearing the minimum."

Rather clever I thought. I said, "You look great," and she smiled triumphantly at Michael.

I was getting fed up with the whole thing between her and the idiot, so I quickly downed the weak Scotch he had given me and said, "Come on, we can't be late."

Then followed a whole explanation about why Madelaine couldn't come too. I was in trouble if Steve Scott blew his big mouth off about open house.

Finally we got out of there and she admired Sammy's E-type. I forgot to mention it wasn't mine, I mean why confuse things? And then we were off.

It suddenly struck me we were much too early to go to the party. I mean nine-thirty would be the earliest we could appear, and then we'd probably be the first anyway.

A nice cozy drink somewhere was the thing. I decided the rooftop bar at the Hilton was suitably romantic. London shimmering and shining below us was a good scene. Or maybe I should destroy her with one of those wild drinks at Trader Vic's.

She was sitting demurely; the ribbon tying back her hair gave her a real little girl look. To tell the truth, I was worried about taking her to Steve's. His parties got very wild—plenty of booze and birds and everyone turning on. I don't go for the pot scene myself—can't see what all the fuss is about—it doesn't do anything for me. Just give me a few Scotches and I'm all right. Of course, in my business, to certain people, I have to pretend I turn on, otherwise they would think I wasn't cool, and you've got to keep a hip image going. Fontaine and friends smoke occasionally. It's like a gang of children having naughty fun. They think they are so decadent. I have found that the really cool pot smokers just get on with it and don't make a whole big group scene. Hal was always high, but he never discussed it.

"It's a shame Madelaine couldn't come," Alexandra said.

"Yeah, sorry about that. Listen, I thought we'd grab a fast drink we're early for the party."

"Oh, what time does it start?" She fiddled with a few of her Victorian frills.

"About nine. Is the Hilton O.K. for you?"

She nodded. "I've never been there."

I was amazed. I'd never met anyone who hadn't been in the Hilton. I took her to the rooftop bar. If she'd never been there, this was something she had to see. The view was a knockout.

I could see she couldn't decide what to drink so I ordered her a champagne cocktail and I had a double Scotch and Coke. We attacked the nuts.

"Have you really never been here?"

"No," she shook her head. "Actually I haven't spent very much time in London at all. Mother hates it, so we never came. But now I've finished school I wanted to come so much and Mother had to agree to let me share a flat with Madelaine—you see Madelaine's mother and mine are best friends."

"What about your father?" I asked.

"Oh, Daddy," she shrugged. "Well, since he married that awful woman, we haven't really spent much time with him." She stopped, then rushed on. "I suppose I shouldn't call her an awful woman, but she is."

If she had stuck her tongue out and added—so there—I wouldn't have been surprised. I wondered what Alexandra would have said if she'd known about Fontaine and me.

She sipped her champagne cocktail and I gulped my Scotch. Her dress didn't reveal any flesh at all, even her arms were covered and the skirt wasn't particularly short.

As if she sensed me thinking this, she said, "Now that I'm in London I must shorten my skirts. I feel like an old frump. In Switzerland we had to wear a regulation skirt length and that was that."

"You don't need your skirt any shorter," I said quickly. Quite frankly, I was fed up to the teeth with all the birds around practically exposing their panties. On a clear night in the club you could see forever. I didn't want Alexandra joining the ranks of the ass flashers. Really, a very short skirt only looks good on a seventeen-year-old flat-chested girl with great legs (thin) —and how many of those were there around? Not many I can tell you.

Alexandra finished her drink. "What time can we go to the party?" she asked brightly.

I glanced at my watch, one of Fontaine's very few presents—Roman numerals, black crocodile strap. It was nearly nine, so I figured it would be all right.

Just as I asked for the check, a loud voice yelled, "Tony, honey pie," and arms were thrown around me. It was Molly Mandy. Just what I needed. She was wearing a multicolored jersey dress cut up everywhere, and as I tried to disentangle myself from her I noticed Alexandra's look of—well—amazement, I guess.

Molly finished her greeting, flashed very white teeth in a friendly smile at Alexandra, winked, said, "Have a ball," laughed and swung off back to her escort, a soberly dressed old man, her speciality. God knows where she found them and God knows why they wanted to be seen out with her.

"Who's that?" Alexandra asked a bit breathlessly.

"Just a girl that comes into the club, a dress designer. Come on."

I took hold of her hand. She went a bit stiff, but didn't pull it away. We set off for the elevator. Oh, if Fontaine could see me now.

I thought I had better cover my tracks. "Listen, you know your father might not approve of me taking you out. I work for him in a roundabout way and he might not like it, so I think it's best not to mention it. Right?"

"All right," she replied, a bit surprised

"I'd like to see a lot more of you," I added quickly. "What do you think?"

What do I think about what?"

I was making a perfect idiot of myself. Never acted so stupid with a girl. The right way to go about it with someone you dig is at the end of the evening to mumble casually, "I'll call you." and then not to call for two weeks. That always gets them going. But I thought this girl was wonderful and sweet and warm and I wanted her to know how I felt. We were outside. "Party time," I said, and helped her into the car.

I was right, we were too early. Steve lounged to the door in his underpants and a sweater.

"Come on in," he said. "Just finished bofing. Where's your bottle?"

I'd forgotten he'd said to bring a bottle.

Carolyn appeared wrapping a pink dressing gown around her. She had nothing underneath and I noticed the firmness of her small breasts and remembered the night we'd had together She was a right raver!

"Tony, you're so bloody cheap," she said. "No bottle indeed. I suppose you forgot." She smiled at Alexandra. "Hi, I 'm Carolyn."

Alexandra smiled back and I noticed her eyes wandering to Steve's crotch. I started a slow burn.

"Make yourselves at home," Steve said. "We're going to dress. Answer the door if it rings."

"Oh, he's terrific," Alexandra whispered when he'd gone.

"Yes, I could see you liked him," I replied dryly, but it was lost on her.

I fixed her a vodka, all I could find. She made a face, but sipped it all the same. I couldn't see any food. Steve was the one that was cheap.

Soon the mob started to arrive. All the familiar faces. What a small town London really is. I spread the word I was off to New York to open a joint. Everyone was suitably impressed. Steve's parties were O.K. when they started; it was only after a couple of hours that they went to rack and ruin.

Alexandra seemed quite happy sitting with her vodka (third one, I aimed to get her smashed).

Steve said to me, "Who's the pussycat?"

Dirty bastard—I hadn't thought she'd be his type. He was chatting her a bit and I was choked. I didn't leave her side, and then who should walk in but "The Twang."

"Ooh, Tony, is that your mother?" she asked in her loud nasal voice. I could have killed her. "You're a lousy son of a bitch," she said in a lower voice, "I could take my choice you know—I don't need you."

Well, why didn't she leave me alone then?

I figured it was time to go. I didn't want Alexandra involved in the coke and pot scene that was starting.

"Come on," I said, "the time has come to find some food."

"I feel awful," she said, "sort of buzzy."

I got her up and she leaned on me. I realized she was loaded—my fault.

Janine said, "Bye-bye, lover boy." She really had a big mouth.

Outside the cold air hit Alexandra like a ton of bricks. She clung to my jacket and said, "I feel sick." Then she was sick, narrowly missing my jacket. Then she started to cry, and I felt like the world's worst shit.

"Please take me home," she moaned.

So much for an evening of fun.

I got her in the car and she huddled miserably on her seat. "I'm so embarrassed," she said weakly. "I've never done anything like that before."

"Don't worry about it," I said. "It happens to everybody. You just had a little too much; you'll soon feel better."

"I'm so sorry." She really was in a state.

"I'll tell you what, we'll go back to my place and I'll fix you some eggs and you can rest up a bit."

She made a face, "I couldn't eat, ugh! I just want to crawl into bed and hide."

Didn't she realize that's just what I had in mind? "Well, how about some coffee then, nice strong black coffee?"

She nodded, and I headed the phallic E-type in the direction of my pad. I switched the car radio on, a touch of Aretha Franklin at her most soulful—very nice. Things are looking up.

We arrived and Alexandra said, "Where are we?"

"My place, going to make you some nice, hot coffee."

"Oh, Tony, I'm being such a bother. I can make coffee, you don't have to go to all this trouble. Just drop me home, and I'll be off your hands."

Was she very smart or a genuine innocent?

I got out of the car and helped her out. "It's no bother."

She looked a bit pale, but being sick had obviously done her good. We stood by the car.

"I'd rather go home," she said, "I'd feel much happier."

"Don't be silly," I was determined to get her to my flat, "you'll feel better after some coffee."

'No, really Tony, I must go home." She started to climb back into the car.

Well. I couldn't stand there arguing all night. Mummy had probably warned her about going to big bad men's apartments. and Mummy was dead right. I got into the car too.

She smiled at me, "You're being very kind."

How could I resist those liquid brown eyes? I took her home. Saw her to the front door, shook her hand (her idea, not mine), kissed her on the cheek (my idea), said good-bye and promised to call her as soon as I got back from New York.

"Great," she said, and was inside her flat with the door closed in my face quick as a flash. Charming!

But she was a lovely little bird, and I could wait.

# 12

# ALEXANDRA

My first day at McLaughton & Co. was awful. To start off with I was late. unforgivable on one's first day; secondly, I felt dreadful. with what I suppose was my first hangover; and thirdly, according to Madelaine all Michael had said about me the previous evening was "What a ridiculous dress."

I wasn't sure that I liked working too much either. I couldn't wait for five o'clock when I could rush home and have a proper chat with Maddy.

Fortunately five o'clock finally came, and I took a taxi home. Maddy was lolling about reading magazines. The lucky beggar didn't start her job until next week.

"What was it like?" she asked. "Have you got a super boss who looks at your legs when you take dictation?"

"No, I've got a grumpy old man who doesn't even know what legs are!"

We both laughed.

"What's for dinner?" I asked. We had planned to take turns organizing meals, and today was Maddy's turn.

"Roast beef and Yorkshire pud, and to start puréed avocado pear, and to finish crème caramel, and we've overspent on our budget, and Michael and Jonathan are coming to dinner. I thought you'd be pleased."

"How did you fix that?"

"Easy. I just asked them. My brother's not one to turn down a free meal."

I was delighted. "What can I wear?" I wailed. Clothes in London were a great problem. I *had* to go shopping.

"Slacks and a tight sweater. Let him see your bosom, maybe *that* will attract him."

I suppose my bosom *was* one of my best features.

I didn't have any tight sweaters, so I borrowed one of Maddy's. It *did* look good.

"Wow!" Maddy said. "Are you wearing a bra?"

"Of course."

"Take if off. Men find it more exciting if you're not."

"I can't do that."

"You want to get him in your evil clutches, don't you?"

I went back into the bedroom, took off my bra, and slipped the sweater back on. You could tell I wasn't wearing one, my breasts bounced when I walked.

Michael and Jonathan came, watched a detective serial on television and devoured every mouthful of the food.

Michael, who had ignored me all evening, finally said, "How was the party last night?"

"It was very nice, but I got a . . ."

Before I could finish, Maddy blurted out, "She's got a date with Steve Scott. He's mad about her."

"You really are seeing London," Michael said grimly, "moving with the in crowd already. I bet your mother won't be too pleased with the company you're keeping."

He was insufferable! They watched a bit more television and then went. I decided I hated him.

Madelaine giggled as soon as they were gone. "It's working," she said. "I think he's jealous."

"He's not, he's *so* sarcastic to me."

"That's good. At least he's *aware* of you now, you're not a little kid he's known for ages any more. And he couldn't take his eyes off your sweater. You'll see; he'll ask you out."

"Do you really think so?" I said, piling up dishes and stacking them in the kitchen.

"Yes, I bet."

We cleared up the mess. I was really exhausted. What with the hangover, the first day at work, and the dinner. I had a bath, brushed my hair and collapsed into bed. I was soon asleep, and dreaming a really awful dream where I appeared at work stark naked and lots of fingers were typing on my body, and then my breasts turned into typewriters, and Michael came and looked at me and turned his back in disgust.

# 13

## TONY

I don't think I've ever met a girl like Alexandra before. She's so sort of innocent and girlish and pretty and soft. She looks great. Clean and tidy and young—I really like her, I really do. Even the thought of New York doesn't turn me on too much and Fontaine doesn't turn me on at all any more. In view of the close relationship involved, I'd be much better off avoiding Fontaine completely. (Impossible!) My only chance is to get away from Hobo and open up on my own. But there's that old problem—money.

I fancy the stewardess wriggling up and down the aisle in tight skirt. I bet she's got something waiting for *her* in New York. Sammy says he's made it on a plane, on a night trip to the south of France. According to him, he had it off with the stewardess in the loo—bit crowded I bet.

"Can I get you anything?" she smiled at me, ignoring the old lady in the seat beside me.

"Yeah, but I don't think it's on the menu."

She giggled, getting the message. These stewardesses weren't slow.

"Do you wish to see the movie?" she smoothed down her tight skirt.

"Any other suggestions?"

Another giggle. "Well, some of the passengers come and sit at the back if they've already seen the film."

There's no doubt about it. I'm irresistible to women! "I'll come and sit at the back then."

"Good." Another smile, and then, wiping it off, she leaned across to the old lady and said briskly, "If you care to see the film it will be sixty pence." I got a whiff of perfume—cheap but sexy.

We had only been in the air an hour, but I reckoned I was going to be all right.

After a decent interval of about three minutes I followed tight skirt to the back of the plane. She was busy with another girl getting out tin foil trays of cold roast beef, congealed potato salad, and hard boiled eggs that had seen better days.

"Need any help?" I asked, trying to squeeze into the tiny kitchen.

"Sorry, you're not allowed in here." She smiled to take away the sting. "You can sit in any of the back seats if you like. I'll be free when the movie starts."

The other girl grinned at me too. She had a suntan and freckles. It looked like it would be a jolly afternoon.

I sat down near the window, viewed the gray expanse of sky and sea and fell asleep.

I was awakened by Miss Tight Skirt sitting beside me. I kept thinking of Sammy's experience. "Ever done a night flight to Nice?" I asked casually.

"Why, yes, as a matter of fact, I used to be on that run."

Oh, no, it couldn't be true!

The movie was on and the plane was pretty dark. We were sitting on the inside two seats of a three-seater, and there was no one across the aisle.

"What's happening?" I asked.

"Anything you like," she replied.

I mean, it had to be the same girl.

I thought of Alexandra so sweet and innocent. I guess I wouldn't be being unfaithful, because nothing had happened with her—yet. I put a hand on the stewardess's knee.

"Oh, come on," she said, "you can do better

than that." She pulled a big regulation rug across us. "Shirley will warn us if anyone comes back to go to the toilet."

What a scene. Under the rug I fought my hand up the tight skirt. She wriggled down in the seat helping me. She had nothing on underneath—making things very easy she was! I unhooked her bra under her prim blouse, her breasts were small but nice, I wished I could see them but there we were all huddled up under the rug.

She unzipped my trousers and with a deft movement twisted herself toward me, and then I was up, up, and away!

"What about the pilots and stewards?" I asked. She was wriggling and squirming at a good pace.

"It's all right, they're all boozing up front," she gasped.

Charming, the pilots are boozing up front, and the stewardess was screwing at the back. I wouldn't travel on *this* airline again!

"Quick, someone's coming," a whispered voice said. It was Shirley, and how right she was.

Oh, boy—fun at twenty-six thousand feet. I was hardly finished when tight skirt pulled out and all in one movement was standing, smoothing her skirt down, and smiling at the passenger who was on his way to the loo.

"Everything all right, sir?"

He nodded. "Er, I'd like a whiskey and soda, is that possible?"

She winked at me, destroyed under the blanket. "Everything's possible on this airline, sir."

She deftly hooked her bra as he went on to the john. "I don't know your name," she said to me, "but I hope you'll fly with us again."

I went back to my seat. There seemed no point in hanging around.

The old lady smiled and nodded to me, "Lovely trip," she said.

"It certainly was!"

"I beg your pardon?"

"Nothing." I slouched down in my seat and watched the end of a silent Doris Day movie. A silent Doris Day is better than a talkative one. Man, I was tired. I fell off to sleep until Miss Tight Skirt appeared, pushing my shoulder and saying, "Fasten your seat belt please, we're coming in to land."

She had freshened up and added a jacket and matching cap. Very smart and efficient.

I yawned and inspected the view. New York was spread out beneath me. What a sight! I wondered what Alexandra was doing now. Poor little chick, getting sick like that. I scribbled her a fast postcard conveniently supplied along with a paper bag to throw up in.

"Dear. A. Dull flight. Had any good vodka lately? See you soon—Tony."

On the way out I handed it to Miss Tight Skirt to post.

"What are you doing tonight?" I asked, more for conversation than anything else.

She gave me a wide grin, "Going out on the town with my fiancé. He's the pilot, you know."

Charming!

I went through Immigration and Customs. An emergency visa had been waiting for me at London airport along with my vaccination certificate. Money can buy anything.

Fontaine was there to meet me, wrapped in mink, shod in crocodile. I was surprised—I didn't think airports were her scene. I forced a smile in her direction. Everyone was taking a second look, she was that kind of a woman.

She wanted me to kiss her, she offered that elegant chiseled face, but I wasn't going to fall for that with everybody looking our way. Benjamin could be having her followed or anything, and I wasn't going to be the patsy.

She said, "How was your trip?"

"Great," I yawned, all my activity was catching up with me! "Saw a movie, boozed a bit. What's all this about anyway?"

She shrugged. "Just an idea of mine."

"Have you got a location or what?"

"Oh, no, we're not that advanced. I thought I

would hear your opinions and see what you think. We can visit all the competition and you can decide if it would be a good idea."

I couldn't help laughing. "You mean all the panic was just for me to look around?"

"Yes, actually it was. I thought you would be thrilled to see New York."

"Yeah, but did I have to leave like a shot out of a gun?"

"Really, Tony, I'm surprised at you. You wanted to come while I was still here, didn't you?"

I nodded. We were in her car by this time and she told the chauffeur to go to her apartment.

"A room has been arranged for you at a hotel," she said, "you can go there after. How's Hobo? Any of my friends been in? Vanessa and Leonard?"

"Haven't seen them."

"Not even her?"

I stared at the lovely Fontaine. What the hell was she getting at? But she smiled sweetly, "What do you think of New York? The city of fairy tales and garbage cans, society balls and riots. You can get anything or do anything here, as long as you have the money, of course. I've got all sorts of exciting things planned for tonight."

I gazed at the view, it was all skyscrapers, rushing people and traffic jams.

What a blast her apartment was! Huge and very modern on the top floor of the tallest building I've ever seen, surrounded by a wild garden with a not-to-be-believed Oriental butler called Adamo who had an English accent and dressed in flowing robes. Too much!

It was the usual scene. Servant bowing and scraping, serving drinks and then vanishing. This one backed out of the apartment with such an inane grin on his face that I thought he would trip over his robe.

"This is great!" I said. "I've never seen anything like it. This view is the end."

"How about this view?"

It was the same Old Fontaine, she was stripping off her clothes and making a grab for me.

Oh, no, after last night, the trip, and her relationship to Alexandra, I didn't know if I could make it. But strength will tell, and I managed to do my best. I felt like a heel, but what could I do? Alexandra wouldn't forgive me for this, but what *could* I do?

My mind was going in sixteen different directions, all the opposite way from the lady under me. "That awful woman," as Alex described her. And she *was* an awful woman. She had dazzled me at first with all her glamour and fame, but now I saw right through her. A social nymphomaniac, that's what she was.

"You're out of practice, Tony." Her voice

was cold and edgy. I finished before she was ready, and she was climbing the walls. Little did she know she was lucky to get anything at all, what with the scene on the plane.

"Yeah, well what do you expect with you away and everything."

"Oh, please, Tony. Let's not play the innocent virgin with each other." She shifted about on the floor. "Finish the job, for God's sake."

I obliged.

This really is a wild city. Great hotels, fantastic TV in the room, with lots of channels. Since the chauffeur brought me here two hours ago I've changed stations ten times. Take your choice—quiz show, old English movie, cowboys and Indians. It's all too much! And about room service, great! Club sandwiches I've only dreamed about. I've ordered three times already.

This is the life. I lay on a king-sized bed after a shower watching a blond chick in a plastic raincoat announce the weather on TV. Fontaine was picking me up at seven, I had an hour yet.

I wanted to phone Alexandra. But Benjamin would be paying the bill and I didn't want him checking through and finding phone calls to his daughter.

I tell you married women disgust me, they're all out for a piece of action away from their husbands. There's hardly one married woman I know that I could truthfully say I couldn't have if I wanted. It makes a man think twice about getting married.

What was I thinking about marriage for anyway? It's not for me, not after all the things I've seen. But if I ever did get married, it would be to Alexandra. My lovely, lovely Alexandra. And she had no money, so where would that be going?

Not that I minded about her having no money—I mean I did think it a bit strong on Benjamin's part—but I had no money either, so I couldn't even think about getting married. Alexandra Blake. Hmmm—not too lyrical, but nice, very nice. I imagined Sadie and Sam's faces if I married a girl that wasn't—"a nice Jewish girl." They would go mad, but so what. I was a big boy now.

The time had come to get dressed. Fontaine had plans for the evening's entertainment—she had reeled off a list of things we were going to do that made me dizzy. We were to start off with a cocktail party, and then go to the apartment of some friends of hers, and then to dinner, and then a round of discotheques, and then there were a couple of other parties we might attend.

I chose my suit carefully. This would be the first time I had been out socially with Fontaine.

I guess under normal circumstances I would be flattered, but things were different now, it all seemed a bit of a drag. It had been quite a day.

I decided on a pale lilac shirt from Turnbull and Asser, handmade, of course. Actually it had been made for Hal, but he didn't like the color, so I bought it. We took the same size in shirts which was useful. He had some great gear which he got fed up with in a hurry—then I would buy it from him at half the original price. He made bread that way because some old dear had probably bought it for him in the first place. Good old Hal. The last of the great promoters!

To go with the shirt I had a toning polka dot tie. The suit was black. With it I wore pearl cufflinks and tie clip; black socks and shoes. Even though I say it myself, I look pretty damn good.

The desk rang to tell me a car was waiting.

Great—New York City here I come!

# 14

# FONTAINE

After Tony left and the chauffeur returned, I went for my massage. Bliss. Hot sweaty hands pounding and pummeling my white skin. Then a delicious steam bath, followed by a soft massage with oil of pine, its odors sinking into my body.

Oh, what luxury—almost as good as sex. Wrapped in pink toweling I had my hair washed, then lay on a floating pink couch while it was dried by concealed jets of air.

This is M'lady's Parlour, the very latest beauty house, and I must say, very impressive.

Sarah dragged me here immediately after I arrived. "It's so divine, darling, you'll come eighteen times."

It's beauty in an aphrodisiac atmosphere. All the boys here are queens, it's like a harem with eunuchs preparing you for the night's fantasy. I thought about Tony. He is still as attractive as ever, that animal something, that eerie night club pallor which contrasts so exciting with his jet black hair. It's a shame he's not a bit more intelligent. Of course if he was he wouldn't be wasting his life away in a discotheque.

Poor Tony. Poor stud. What will happen to him when his hard body and curly hair are gone? Who will want him then? As a matter of fact after his performance today I would say he was not in good form at all.

Roger did my hair, petite Roger with a mass of golden curls and pursed bitchy lips. "Darling, do you believe what Clarissa wore to the premiere last night? She looked like a yellow baby elephant! Ridiculous! My friend says her dress was a Rudy Gernreich, but I can't believe that Rudi would be so wicked."

I smiled. The good thing about Roger was the fact that one could relax and listen to all the gossip. His bitcheries could go on forever.

He continued, "Saw a dreadful movie last night. I couldn't believe the clothes though, terribly now. You'd look divine in white satin with lots of fox fur. I think I'm going to do your hair Grecian. Strand it with pearls and things."

I felt so good from the massage, my body

tingled. Oh, God, if all these little twits could see Tony they'd cream themselves!

He was getting a rather attractive quality of self-confidence. With me he had always been so fawning and adoring, now he seemed to treat me in a slightly cooler fashion. Although of course he was still a boy scout when it came to material things. Why the way his mouth had popped open when he saw my apartment! The stud prowling around and sniffing the luxury!

Of course, I know eventually he will begin to flap his wings, but I'm sure this trip will cool him down and make him realize exactly who he's mixing with. After all, there aren't many women like me around, and however many little affairs he has to indulge in he'll soon find that out.

Roger did wonders with my hair. Only two pieces and it really looks marvelous.

"Have a lovely time," he said stepping back to admire his work.

I went home and phoned Sarah, we were all to dine together. I hadn't told her about Tony. I had just said a business associate of Benjamin's was joining us. I couldn't wait to see her face!

"What are you wearing?" she asked.

"I haven't decided yet," I replied, although I was going to wear the backless black silk Cardin.

"Neither have I." What a liar she was.

"We'll see you about eight. Going to pop into the Carltons' party first."

"What a bore. They're so show business, Alan can't stand them."

Actually I knew that Sarah and Alan hadn't been invited, as Salamanda Smith, a Hollywood film star, and Alan had been a very hot item indeed the previous summer, and Peter Carlton, whom she had since married, was terribly jealous. Oh, the intricacies of the social set!

"Are the Bells and Sidwells meeting at your place too?"

"Yes, everything's arranged." Sarah lowered her voice, "I had a wonderful afternoon. Have you ever tried yoga?"

I didn't want to get involved in one of Sarah's sexual discussions, they always began with a lowered voice.

"Yes, darling, often. See you later." I hung up.

# 15

# TONY

Fontaine is the biggest put-down merchant of all time. Here I am, looking great, feeling great, ready to go, and she gives me one of those tight little smiles of hers and says, "Tony, darling, we'll simply have to stop and get you a decent tie. You just can't go out like that." I mean screw her, sitting there with her hair looking like a Carnival Queen. Who does she think she is? She doesn't own me, and pretty soon she's going to find that out.

She dragged me into some store and lumbered me with six of the worst ties you could imagine. Imported yet, probably couldn't find a buyer for them in their own country.

I put on the best of the bunch to keep her

happy, and silently fumed. Fontaine was a cow. An old cow. I contemplated telling her to take a running jump, but I had no money to pay the hotel and I'm sure if I did that, no job to return to in good old Blighty.

Mrs. Khaled had me by the short and curlies, and what was worse she bloody well knew it.

We arrived at the party, it was pretty jammed, but everyone turned to take a look at us. Fontaine hadn't bothered to tell me whose party it was, but I soon got the message when Salamanda Smith, *the* Salamanda Smith, came waltzing over.

She was a gorgeous bird, curvy and blond with a pair of boobs that fairly knocked your eyes out. I'd just seen her in a wild desert movie, a full-of-sex-and-sand type thing. She was bowled over by Fontaine, but I could see she had an eye (baby blue) for me, and we got to chatting about her last movie.

She had to go to greet some more people and Fontaine had done a vanish, so there I was on my own. I scouted around and got hold of a Scotch from a white-coated guy who called me "Bud" and was really loaded. Was he a waiter? The way he was acting I wasn't quite sure. But he picked up a tray, belched and set off in the direction of some guest, so I guessed he was.

He weaved into a fake marble column, and it swayed, but stood its ground, then he staggered with his tray over to some people and hands stretched out like vultures relieving him of the glasses. He came rolling back in my direction— "S'elluva party," he mumbled, "lotsa booze." Then he was off again toward Salamanda, and, dropping his tray with a loud crash, he grabbed hold of her with one hand, and with the other unzipped his fly and said, "Get a load of this, honey!"

There was a short silence while she struggled to free herself. Then three guys jumped on the waiter.

It was a funny scene, really. Salamanda took a deep breath, smiled, and the waiter was dragged, blood dripping from his face, out of the room. Great! I counted to ten knowing that Fontaine would appear at my side, anxious to hear all.

Fontaine—the last of the great gossips. She was there on the stroke of nine. "What happened?" her silver-lidded eyes glistened anxiously.

"Just some drunk waiter, nothing exciting."

"Oh," she was disappointed, "is that all."

Salamanda was now retelling the story to a small group surrounding her, and Fontaine went over. I trailed behind. She was just saying, "and there was his enormous *thing!* Just staring me in the face!"

Fontaine shot me a dirty look. I'd left out the best bits.

I wished I could phone Alexandra. I looked around for a phone, nobody would notice me making a quick call to London with this group. I strolled out of the door, looked about and found an empty bedroom with a shiny gold bedside model. I grabbed it quick, "Overseas please—London England—a personal call to Miss Alexandra Khaled—8934434. No I'll hang on."

A beautiful girl came into the room, long straight black hair, long black body. She looked directly at me, "You going to Marcello's after?"

"Who's Marcello?"

Her eyes were stony, unsmiling. "You putting me on?"

"Nope," I shook my head and winked. "Who is he? I'm a stranger here." "Ah, God Almighty." she smoothed down her long black hair, "Marcello's is a restaurant, man, everyone seems to be going there, I'm looking for someone to take me. You interested?"

I was interested all right, but unavailable. "I'm with someone. How about another night?"

Her eyes swept over me. "Yeah, maybe."

Just then the operator said, "I'm putting you through now, your party's on the line."

Then Alexandra's voice, clear and sweet, "Hello?"

The girl was combing her hair at a mirror.

"Hello, baby, and how are you today?"

"Oh, Tony, how nice of you to phone me all the way from America. I'm much better, thank you. I feel such an idiot about last night."

A warm glow came over me, "Don't give it another thought. It was my fault for taking you to a lousy party like that. What are you doing?"

"I'm in bed actually."

I imagined her with brushed shining hair and a fluffy pink nightdress. "That's the best place to be." I glanced over at the girl. She was hanging around. I covered the mouthpiece of the phone, "Write down your number," I hissed at her. I said back into the phone, "I miss you."

I did miss her. The girl wrote Norma and a number on a book of matches and threw them at me, then she went out.

There was silence from Alexandra. "I said I miss you."

"I know," her voice was a whisper.

"Well?"

"Well what?"

"Do you miss me?"

"I don't know. I mean you've only been gone a day, and after all we don't know each other very well." She paused. "Yes, I do miss you."

My heart did a little skip, "I'm going to be back soon, then we'll get to know each other really well. Be a good girl."

"Yes," she had such a lovely accent.

"See you soon." I hung up. It was good to be

alive. I peered at myself in the mirror. I looked good, but wished I had a suntan. Maybe Fontaine would fancy a few days in Florida.

I went back to the party and found Fontaine. She was holding court, her clipped British tones ringing around the room. When she paused for air, she noticed me, "Oh, there you are, we've got to be going." She wasn't as friendly toward me as she had been. You never knew with Fontaine, she blew hot and cold. Maybe she didn't like having me out with her, maybe she thought I wasn't good enough. All right for a fuck, but not for her friends. I scowled. She glared. We left.

In the car she said testily, "You know, Tony, you shouldn't act so star-struck. I would have thought that by now you would have been used to meeting celebrities."

*Me—star-struck!* I was choked! That was the *last* thing I was.

She tapped talonlike nails on her small gold (real, of course) handbag, and added, "You made a fool of yourself with Salamanda. You acted like a film fan. Don't you realize five years ago she was a stripper, and you—anyone—could have had her for ten dollars."

I've learned one lesson in life. Never argue with a woman when she's putting down another woman.

"Yeah, you're right," I conceded. Who needed an argument?

She softened a bit. "Just don't forget—you'll probably meet many big stars while you're here. Don't mention their work or anything about it, socially that's just not on."

Silly cow! I yawned. "I'd love to go to Florida."

She ignored me.

We arrived at a big apartment house, and the doorman nearly broke his neck getting her ladyship out of the car.

"These are my dearest friends in New York," Fontaine said, "Sarah and Alan Grant, a wonderful couple. Don't embarrass me."

I mean, what did she think I was going to do—pee on the carpet or something?

We went into a fantastic pad on the ground floor. Big, dark, crammed with antiques, stuffed animals and tall plants. Very nice. What a scene you could have here!

This lady came to greet us, bony face, pulled-back black hair and whiter than white skin. She looked like she was suffering from a touch of malnutrition. She and Fontaine kissed, summing up each other's outfits with their eyes. Then Fontaine said, "Sarah, I want you to meet Tony. Benjamin sent him over."

Man, she made me sound like a package! Sarah looked me over. She had wild black eyes that burned right through you. Her lips were thin and painted dark red. I guessed she must be about forty. If you like skeleton-thin older birds, she was a knockout. Personally I don't. Her glance jumped between me and Fontaine, and she smiled slightly. "Well, what a surprise."

Fontaine smiled too. "Yes," she said, and they linked arms and walked over to the bar, leaving me standing there like an idiot.

There were four or five other people sitting about, and a guy got up and came over to me. He had what women's magazines would call a craggy, handsome face. He wore a shapeless gray suit. "Alan Grant," he said, shaking hands and giving me an amused squint.

"Tony Blake."

"Come and have a drink." He took me over to the bar and fixed me a very large Scotch on the rocks. He fixed himself an even bigger one and disposed of it in three hefty gulps. Then he made himself another and said, "Who are you?"

Charming! I mean I love questions like that from a complete stranger. What do you say? The Pope—Gunga Din—"I'm over here for Benjamin Khaled looking for—er—properties."

"Oh. Are you having an affair with the lovely Mrs. Khaled then?"

I mean, was I supposed to hit him or what? Fortunately Fontaine came over. "Alan, you naughty boy, what are you saying?"

She was flirting, a pose of hers that drove me mad.

He laughed. "Nothing. How are you my sweet?"

"I'm fine." Their eyes met in the sort of intimacy usually reserved for lovers. They probably were. That would just about be Fontaine's scene, knocking off her best friend's husband. I didn't care. My little Alexandra was tucked up at home in bed, and that's all I cared about.

Sarah took my arm. "Come, Tony, I want you to meet the others."

I racked my brain to find out where I'd seen her before. I pride myself on never forgetting a face, and I knew I'd seen this one somewhere. She hadn't been in the club, that I was sure of. She was certainly very striking, although, as I said before, not my type at all. Her hand was brittle on my arm, skeleton fingers digging in. Suddenly it struck me where I knew her from. *Vogue* magazine, three months ago, a big layout of her in Bermuda or somewhere, modeling beach exotica. I told you I have a great memory. Sarah Grant—society bigwig—New York City.

"Fontaine never told me about you," she said in a deep, husky voice, "you're divine."

Instant lay, better watch out, didn't want to upset her ladyship.

I was then introduced to the others, your average rich couples—neither of the women could hold a candle to Fontaine or Sarah, and the men were balding and moved in a cloud of cigar smoke.

After some boring small talk we left, a convoy of chauffeured cars.

First stop was dinner, an exclusive restaurant off Fifth Avenue, with hothouse plants growing wild, and gold-jacketed waiters. I sat between Fontaine and Sarah, fighting a losing battle to taste my food against the fumes of their respective perfumes.

They both ignored me, making polite small talk around the rest of the table. I couldn't join in as I didn't know who or what they were talking about. I mean are you ready for "Fleur met Itsy in St. Moritz and they had a terrible fight and he ended up with Poopsie at Mooey's." Alan was the only one who spoke to me. I had a feeling he was as bored as I was.

So this was New York—social circuit number one. You can have it and shove it.

Dinner dragged on and on and I was getting a bad case of yawning. At last Fontaine said, "I think we'd better get Tony to Pickett's before he falls asleep on us." She shot me a dark look to let me know she was furious about my yawning all night.

Pickett's was the newest disco to open and make it big. I had heard about it, but all the same it was a shock. The whole interior of the club was like a huge monster's open mouth. Fangs and cobwebs hung from everywhere, and in a transparent tooth hanging like a light fixture from the ceiling, a near-naked female freaked out to the blaring sound of James Brown. There was an assortment of waitresses dressed in flimsy bits of cobwebs and lots of glimpses, of a tit here, an ass there. Pretty wild, but not what I'd call a cool scene. I mean who needs gimmicks? The customers are supposed to make the fun.

Fontaine made her usual grand entrance, and the guy running the joint nearly kissed her feet. He was small, dark and nervous looking. No competition there.

We were seated around a table shaped like a huge withered hand, and a little teeny bopper, happy in her cobweb gear, took our order. Champagne all around and a Scotch for me. "Why fight it," Alan murmured. "Why not get used to her habits?"

"I only drink Scotch," I answered.

"Come on, Alan sweetie, let's show 'em." Fontaine was getting frisky as she dragged Alan off to dance.

"Shall we?" Sarah asked with arched eyebrows, already getting up without waiting for my reply.

I followed her to the dance floor. She did an even more embarrassing dance than Fontaine.

What the hell was I doing here? Six months before I would have given anything to be involved in this scene with these people, in fact I wouldn't have believed it was possible. But now—well, who needed it? I had everything going for me in London, I didn't need this trailing-behind-Fontaine bit.

We stayed at Pickett's an hour, and then went on to The Flower Mission, a wild mass of psychedelic symbols and freak-out light effects.

By this time the other two couples had dropped out and it was just Fontaine, Sarah, Alan and me against the world. We were all well smashed.

"Have you ever studied yoga?" Sarah asked me, black eyes piercing and probing.

"Er—no."

"You should. You have a powerful body. I'm sure you would excel at it."

"Tony," Fontaine said excitedly. "Alan's met a man here who can get us some cigarettes." Her voice lowered on the word cigarettes and I knew with a sinking feeling she meant pot. That's all I needed, one of her aren't-we-being-wicked pot-smoking scenes. I just don't dig it, it doesn't do a thing for me except make me go to sleep, and from the way Fontaine is carrying on, me going to sleep is not what she has in mind.

"We'll go to Sarah and Alan's, shall we?" Not so much as a question, more a statement.

So we left and chauffeured all the way to the Grant pad.

Once there the two women disappeared and

Alan made a beeline for the bar. He wasn't talking, just knocking back a large glass of brandy and looking hollow-eyed.

"So, what's the action?" I asked, helping myself to a drink as he didn't seem to be offering.

"God knows," he said. "You're lucky, at least you're not married to yours."

What did *that* mean?

I glanced at my watch. It was three A.M. I was bushed. I tried to calculate what time it was in London. Five hours difference but I couldn't remember which way.

Sarah came back in first. She had changed into a full-length brocade caftan, and her jet black hair was combed straight down. She looked vaguely Indian.

Fontaine followed, hair still piled high on her head, but she had changed into a long white floating thing, slightly transparent, and I could see the outlines of her small naked breasts.

"Alan," Sarah said, "why don't you and Tony put these on?" She handed us each a sort of short black silk kimono.

"Come on," Alan said resignedly.

I followed him into another room, and he stripped off his clothes and put on the black kimono.

He smiled grimly, "I know why I'm doing this, how about you?"

I felt uptight about the whole thing, but what

the hell, in a way it was rather exciting. I put on the kimono, the silk felt great. I wished it wasn't so short, it just about covered my balls!

We went back inside. Fontaine and Sarah were smoking already, taking long thin-lipped drags. I went to sit beside Fontaine, but she motioned me over to Sarah. Oh, boy—if the regulars could see me now!

There was some weird Japanese music playing, and Sarah offered me her cigarette. I took a drag. We were sitting on a sofa, and opposite on another sofa were Fontaine and Alan.

I handed the cigarette back to Sarah. She puffed and leaned back blowing little smoke rings to the ceiling.

My turn, this wasn't too bad, I felt a certain numbness creep over me and the music sounded fantastic. I put the cigarette back in her mouth, and she leaned over and put her hands under the kimono. Her fingers felt like burning tongs as they fled around my flesh.

I glanced over at Fontaine. She was lying against the cushions and Alan was peeling the white thing off her. I watched, fascinated, as her body came into view and he started to kiss her. Her legs were spread and she moaned softly.

Meanwhile Sarah's hands manipulated me. She took off my kimono, and man, I felt great! Then I started to fly and I was pounding into someone and when I looked it was Fontaine and then Sarah and then both of them were all over me. It was a kaleidoscope of faces, and for the first time I was really stoned.

I opened my eyes and I was in my room at the hotel lying on top of the bed with all my gear on. How did I get back?

That bloody bitch Fontaine was a real balls breaker, and her skinny friend—Miss No Tits society bag. All right, so we'd had a big scene and there wasn't a gun at my head, but how could I have done it? What about Alexandra? What about Sadie and Sam, my nice old parents? What if they ever knew, could see? I've always had this funny sort of thought that after you die you sit in a room and like watching a movie your whole life plays across the screen and all the people you know get to watch it. Charming! Last night's scene would make lovely viewing. Shit! Making it with Fontaine is one thing, but having a show with her so-called friends is another.

That faggot husband of Sarah's tried to sneak it in while the two women crawled all over me. But I caught him at that little game, thank you very much. I remember Fontaine saying, "Let him do it, Tony, you'll love it." Bitch! She was *really* stoned.

It was two o'clock and I was starving. I had a shower and ordered three eggs and a hamburger from room service. What was I supposed to do?

Hang around until her ladyship decided to call me? I watched television. Maybe I should call the club later. Maybe I should call Alexandra now. What the fuck am I doing here anyway? It's a long way from the Elephant and Castle. I guess I fell asleep again, because when I woke up the TV screen was alive with sweaty teenagers and the phone was ringing.

"Yeah?"

"My, my. Aren't we American already!"

I glanced quickly at my watch, five-fifteen, and she was only just calling. "What's happening?" I asked.

"Well, darling, all sorts of exciting things. Did you enjoy last night?"

"No."

Her voice went very cold. "Oh—why?"

"It's not my scene, Fontaine. I don't like threesomes, or foursomes. What's wrong with normal sex?"

Her laugh was amused. "Tony, you are *such* a little—or should I say big—suburbanite. It was fun. If you relaxed, it could be a lot more fun."

"I don't want to do it again. O.K.?"

Her voice was sarcastic. "*Yes, sir.* We will not indulge in any more naughty little orgies."

There was silence. I knew she hated being criticized, but God Almighty, somebody had to tell her. It was bad enough screwing around on her husband, but this beat the band.

"What's happening?" I asked.

"I don't want to corrupt you, Tony dear, but I thought you might like to come over for an hour or so, then there are two parties and dinner with Sarah and Alan."

Oh, Christ! I certainly didn't want to face Sarah and Alan again. What were we all supposed to do—discuss positions?

"Look, I don't want to see them. I'll come to the parties with you, then maybe I'll roam around on my own, get the feel of things."

"Tony, you can be such a bore! All right then, do that. Be here in a half-hour." She slammed the phone down.

How did I ever get myself into this?

It was too early to phone the club, but Alexandra should be home. Was it a clever move to risk a phone call? No.

I thought of her pretty wide-eyed face and her soft auburn hair. She was the sort of girl who would still look good in ten or even twenty years. I decided that when I got back to London I would take her down to the Elephant and Castle and introduce her to Sadie and Sam. What a shock they'd get to see me with such a lovely girl. They thought I only went out with showgirls and "tarty bits of fluff" as Sadie always said. How many times had they both said to me—find yourself a nice Jewish girl and settle down. So what difference Jewish smooish, as long as she was nice. They would love pretty little Alex.

I got dressed. Polo-necked striped silk shirt, one of Hal's best buys, and my Dougie Hayward gray suit. I had to get some money from Fontaine. I was walking around with nothing. It was embarrassing, especially if I was going to take off on my own later.

On top of the TV with my comb and cigarettes were several books of matches I had picked up at various joints the previous evening. I liked things like that, lay them around the London pad and people knew you had traveled. Scribbled across the front of "Lorenz—eat in style" was the name Norma and a number.

Norma? I didn't know a Norma. Come to think of it I'd never been to a place called Lorenz either.

Norma, Norma, Norma. Ah, yes, the tall black lady with the long black hair at the party last night. Rather beautiful, a definite raven, very cool. I dialed the number and a guarded, tired voice answered "Yeah?"

"Is Norma there?"

"Wait a minute, I'll see. Who is it?"

"Tony Blake, but she doesn't know my name. We met at a party we . . ."

"Hold it, baby, I don't want your life history."

The guarded voice left me hanging on while I strained to hear the muffled conversation at the other end. Then a voice identical to the first one said, "Yeah?"

"Norma?"

"Yeah."

"We met at Salamanda Smith's party last night." Nothing like dropping a name. "I was on the phone in the bedroom, remember?"

"Yeah."

She was a wild conversationalist. "I thought I could see you later, like buy you a drink or something?"

"Sounds O.K. I'm having dinner with some guys, you can join us if you like."

"Some guys" didn't sound too exciting. "Well, look, if you're busy, maybe another night."

"Suit yourself. We'll be at Marcello's if you change your mind."

She hung up. Friendly girl, couldn't care less if I came or not.

I didn't even have cab fare, so I walked the few blocks to Fontaine's. She let me in herself, her hair hanging smoothly down her back, her face a mess of white cream but her eyes fully made up. She wore a thin silk dressing gown.

"Come into the bedroom. I'm making up. Fix the champagne first: it's in the fridge."

I went into the fully fitted oak-paneled kitchen and opened several cupboards before locating the refrigerator which was cleverly disguised as part of the wall.

I opened the champagne and took it into the bedroom. Fontaine was lying on the bed, the silk dressing gown exposing her from the waist down so that the whole view looked slightly obscene.

"We won't need glasses," she whispered. "Just bring the bottle; we'll drink it my way."

I was excited in spite of myself. She repulsed me, but my body was responding to her. I took off my suit and shirt, I certainly wasn't spoiling the outfit.

"Come on Tony," she said impatiently. "I'm thirsty."

When it was all over the room stunk of champagne. I lay on her bed watching her calmly get on with her makeup. I knew I couldn't make it any more. Oh, I could "make it" in the physical sense, no problems there, but after—well, I get this kind of unclean feeling, this feeling of shame. With other women there's always some affection—something—even if it's just a casual lay. But Fontaine is cold as bloody ice, it's almost as if she's just using my body to suit herself. She's a bitch, and I've got to get away from her. Especially now with Alexandra in the picture.

"Can I shower?" I asked.

"Of course, you don't have to ask permission. Use the one in the guest room." She was painting her thin lips and didn't look up.

I showered the smell of champagne off me

and the smell of Fontaine, and then I just stood there, turning the water on to icy cold. It felt good.

When I got back to London I was going to find someone to back me in a new club. It shouldn't be that difficult. I had a lot of connections, and me in a new club couldn't fail. I mean I'm not being conceited but Hobo would never have made it without me. Maybe the new place could be called Tony's, or is that too obvious? I like it myself, sounds good. Find a location, find a backer and kiss Fontaine Balls-Breaker Khaled good-bye.

"Tony, are you ready?" She walked in wearing black satin and lots of diamonds. She looked annoyed. "What the hell are you *doing* in here?"

I got out of the shower quick, skin shriveled by the cold.

"Come on, for God's sake. I hate hanging around waiting." She swept out of the room.

I dressed quickly and found her on her terrace, smoking.

"Listen, since we'll be splitting up later I'd better have some money," I said. "I was rushed over here so quickly I couldn't arrange any."

"I see." She looked furious. I knew she hated parting with cash. "Why on earth didn't you ask Benjamin's secretary?"

"I didn't meet her. The whole thing was arranged by phone."

She opened her small evening bag and extracted three ten dollar bills. "That's all I have," she said. "I'll make some arrangements for you tomorrow."

Charming! Thirty measly dollars to see New York on. That wasn't going to get me very far.

We went to the first party. It was held in a restaurant and the crush was terrible. I stood by the door watching Fontaine waft around. I drank three Scotches.

After a half-hour she found me, gripped my arm and said, "We're leaving. Do see if you can be a little more sociable at the next party. Klaus is coming with us."

Klaus turned out to be a small gay dressmaker, dressed to kill in frills, with rotting teeth and beady eyes. He sat between me and Fontaine in the car, pressing his thigh close to mine.

"Klaus has taken New York by storm with his thirties trouser-suits," Fontaine remarked.

Well, good for little old beady-eyed Klaus. He may have taken New York by storm, but he was going to get a punch on the nose if he pressed his leg against mine any harder.

The second party was even worse. A party full of queers. Droves of them. Scattered among them were the well-dressed ladies, and a few—very few—normal guys. At least they looked normal.

Klaus said, "How divine. Everyone's here."

Fontaine said, "All the best designers in New York. You'd better stay close to me Tony, I know how you feel about your precious ass!"

I hated her. So beautiful and elegant and bitchy.

I stayed there about ten minutes, but I was getting so many leers and coy glances I couldn't stand it any longer.

"I'm getting out of here," I told Fontaine.

She brushed me aside with a cool, "Bye-bye," and I wandered out into the New York night.

It was still early, before nine, and I tried to decide if it was too early to try Marcello's. I was starving, with gnawing pains in my stomach. I walked into a hamburger joint and had three. That felt a lot better. What now? Seek out the wild-looking Norma? There seemed to be nothing else to do. I hopped a cab and told him Marcello's and he knew where it was.

From the outside it looked all right. Small red and white awning, a few steps down, a pretty girl at the reception desk. She smiled at me. "You 'ave reservation, sir?" She was Italian. Should have known it when I saw those great big eyes.

"I thought I'd have a drink."

"Certainly sir—downstairs." She smiled again. I smiled. If Norma didn't show—I wondered what time this little darling finished.

Downstairs it was packed. The bar bordered the restaurant and every table was full. Imagine Hobo on a Saturday and you have the scene. I ordered a Scotch and looked for Norma.

She was easy to spot with her sleek black hair in a long braid, and huge, horn-rimmed, tinted glasses on her nose. She was at a table with three guys. I watched them a bit before going over. She was a very striking girl, her eyes big and soulful.

"Hi there," she said. She was authoritative. With a snap of her fingers she got a waiter to bring another chair. She nodded around the table: "Mark—Terry—Davy—this is Tony." Two of the guys were white, the other was a very good-looking black with a beard.

"Hi man," the bearded Davy greeted me.

The whole thing was a very warm scene. I could relax. Norma surveyed me coolly through her tinted lenses. "Hey, what were you doin' at that awful party? What a giant-sized drag!"

I nodded. "Somebody took me."

"Yeah, somebody took you all right." She laughed. "First time in my life I ever got stood up. Some guy was supposed to meet me there, but the bum never showed!"

"That will teach you to go out with stars, girlie," Davy said, grinning.

"You can bet on that," Norma agreed. "Now to beat the band the guy's secretary—secretary yet, hasn't even got the balls to call me himself—phones me today and says—I quote—'Mr. Nicholas is so sorry he couldn't manage last night. May I confirm your address as Mr. Nicholas wishes to send you a color television set.' Man I laughed and laughed. 'Tell Mr. Nicholas to take his color TV and shove it right up his rude white ass,' I said."

Everyone laughed.

"That guy is too much," Norma continued. "He can only make it with black girls. He has some kind of hang-up, can't make it with a white lady. Then the poor guy thinks he has to pay. I've got a little news for him—if I was planning on getting paid, a color TV wouldn't go anywhere near covering the cost! I should never have balled him, but he's so beautiful—umm—that body—wowee!"

Buck Nicholas was a very famous movie actor, who usually appeared in tattered tee shirts and tight Levis to show off his equally famous body.

"You know, we've met before last night," Norma said, lifting her glasses, balancing them in her hair, and staring at me.

"We did?" I couldn't remember, and I had a good memory.

"Yeah, Hobo, London. You used to run the joint, all the little girlies creaming themselves over you."

I was sure I could never forget meeting a girl like Norma.

"I still run Hobo. When was it?"

"Coupla months back—you wouldn't remember me. I was wearing a blond wig. You came over. I was with Steve Scott."

Bingo! Could I ever forget her. What a night *that* had been, with every guy in the place fighting to meet her and Steve playing it cool.

"Of course! You look completely different now."

"Yeah—I only use the blond wig when I want to really knock 'em in the aisles. I was only in London two days, crazy city, I'm going back soon. What are you doing here?"

"Might open up a Hobo here. I'm getting the feel of things."

"Yeah? Great. Talk to Davy, he can *really* show you the town."

She was right. After dinner ( I just drank) Terry and Mark went off, and Norma, Davy and I saw New York. But I mean *really* saw it. We went all over in Davy's silver Porsche—uptown, downtown, Harlem, Chinatown. Norma was a wonderful girl. She talked non-stop in her laconic style, and she danced like a mother, and she laughed a lot and drank a lot, and at SIX A.M. exhausted, drunk, and happy we landed at her apartment.

"Hey, you're really somethin'," she said laughing and undoing her jet black plaited hair until it hung straight to her waist.

"You're not bad yourself," I replied, putting my arms around her and pulling her close to me.

We were both loaded and both in the same happy mood. She was almost as tall as me, and I'm six one. She had on a clingy orange dress which I helped her out of. Underneath there was a gorgeous brown skin and nothing else.

She laughed and moved out of my arms. "Want a drink?"

"Yeah, great." I watched her move about the room, pouring two Scotches and clinking the ice. She had a fantastic body, like a long, supple panther.

I felt a little twinge of guilt about Alexandra, but this lady was so *beautiful!* A man can only take so much temptation.

She came over to me and held the drink to my lips. I caught hold of one of her wild boobies. She took the drink away from me and put it carefully on the table.

"You want to swing, man—let's swing. I've got a wild bedroom. Only no hang-ups, huh?"

I covered her ass with my hands. "No hang-ups."

"O.K. Let's go!" She turned around and I followed her, my hands sticking to her backside, so high and round like a boy's.

Her bedroom was great. Leopard-skin walls and a huge circular bed with a giant blowup of Mick Jagger (Mick Jagger??) on the ceiling. She pressed a button, and Ray Charles singing "Eleanor Rigby" flooded the room.

I pushed her onto the bed and she stared up at me with amused black cat's eyes as I got undressed. I pinned her shoulders to the bed. I started to kiss her, and we started to swing and I could have sworn Mick Jagger's eyes moved! moved!

I left her asleep at eleven the next morning, and cabbed it back to my hotel. There was a message for me. "Please be ready to leave on noon plane for London. All tickets etc. to be collected at Kennedy Airport, information desk. Alice Clerk—secretary for Benjamin Al Khaled."

Charming! I was on the move again.

# 16

## FONTAINE

Reflecting on the whole thing, I concluded it was a dreadful mistake. I should have left Tony where he was, he is nothing but an embarrassment here.

From the moment he arrived three days ago he has been gauche, naive, star-struck and a bore. Of course there was that one fun evening when we all got high, but he had the nerve to lecture me the next day about how I shouldn't involve myself in orgies, and that he certainly wasn't going to do it again. I mean, really, as far as I can remember he enjoyed it more than anyone! Sarah thinks he's a bore. "All cock and no brains!" she says. "Really Fontaine, find yourself an Oriental."

She is right. The stud is a dismal failure in New York. I have arranged for him to leave on the noon flight and this time I am *not* going to the airport.

Benjamin is flying in anyway. Dear rich Benjamin.

There are a lot of things I need at Tiffany's. Also I have seen a beautiful sable coat. And Saks has some divine Rudi Gernreich orignals. Benjamin is arriving at the perfect time.

The phone rang and I waited for Adamo to announce who it was.

"Mr. Blake, madam."

"Tony, darling." I may as well say good-bye with charm, the poor stud was probably shattered.

"Look Fontaine, I just received a message that I'm supposed to be leaving."

"Yes, darling. Benjamin's coming into town, and I think you've seen enough to form some opinions. There's no point in you being away from Hobo too long."

"Yeah, well I suppose you're right. But I mean I'm shuttled around like luggage. Why didn't you mention it last night?"

"Oh, don't be boring, Tony. I didn't know last night. Anyway, do give everyone my love, especially Vanessa. I'm sure you'll see Vanessa." Oh, God, he probably couldn't wait.

"Yeah, I'll see you in London then."

"Ciao, sweetie."

That's got rid of him. Back to his little London dollies. He's so narrow-minded and suburban. After all I've taught him, he still only likes one position! Stupid boy.

The phone again. "Mr. Grant, madam."

"Alan, darling."

"How about meeting today?"

"Where's Sarah?"

"Out. Well? Two o'clock at the Plaza?"

"No, that's too late, Benjamin's coming in this afternoon. How about the St. Regis at one?"

"Fine, I'll arrange it."

"Alan."

"Yes?"

"Bring your imagination."

He laughed. Dear Alan wasn't so bad, not as equipped as Tony, but passable. After the little *ménage à quatre* of the other evening, I was really rather fond of him. It would be a pleasant way to pass the day until Benjamin arrived.

# 17

## ALEXANDRA

My second day at McLaughton & Co. was no better than the first. I don't think I can stick it out at this job. Tony phoned me from New York last night. Maddy was very impressed. "Wait until Michael finds out both Tony *and* Steve Scott are after you," she said. "He'll be green."

When I got home Maddy was a mass of Carmen rollers and face cream. "I've got a date," she announced, all pleased with herself. "Jonathan phoned to thank me for the fabulous dinner last night, and asked me to a movie."

"Great," I said with as much enthusiasm as I could muster. "What about Michael?"

She looked guilty. "Oh, sorry, Alex, Jonathan

didn't mention him. But I promise I'll pump him tonight and get all the info. You know, what girls he sees and everything like that. It will be very useful to know all those things."

"Yes, very." I was acutely miserable.

Madelaine spent the next hour doing herself up and singing and generally being far too cheerful.

"Stay out of the way when Jonathan gets here," she said. "I'll tell him you're at some amazing party."

"Thanks," I said, shutting myself in the bedroom with a tin of cold baked beans. I heard the doorbell and a mumble of voices and then the door slammed, and I was alone. I phoned Mummy. I wished I was at home.

"Why don't you bring some friends down with you this weekend?" Mummy said. "We could all go riding."

"Perhaps I will. Can I let you know?"

I decided to invite Michael, whether Maddy thought it was a good idea or not. I didn't like being in the flat alone. I suppose this is the bad thing about living away from home. I even felt nervous, sort of kept on hearing funny noises as it got later and darker.

I drew all the curtains, turned on the television and concentrated on a play. Then the phone rang.

"Is Alexandra there?" A husky mysterious voice.

"This is she."

"Steve Scott. How are you?"

"Oh—I'm fine. How are you?" I felt myself blushing.

"All right. Sort of driftin' along like a good boy. I thought you might want to come out."

"Now?" I blushed even deeper.

"I sort of thought tomorrow night, like dinner and that bit. You want to?"

"Oh, yes, I'd like to." Wait until Michael hears about this!

"All right then, why don't you come over about nine?"

"Great!"

"See you then."

"Just a second," I said, frantically searching for a pencil and paper. "Could you please tell me your address."

He did so, added "Don't dress up," and was gone.

How terrific! Although I would sooner it was Michael. I couldn't wait to see Maddy's face!

She staggered in looking awful. She reminded me of how I had felt Sunday night. It was quite late, but I had purposely stayed up reading.

"Alex, I think I'm going to be sick!" she announced.

"Well, for goodness' sake, make sure it's in the bathroom."

It was, and like me she felt better afterward. She lay on top of her bed groaning and I made some tea.

"I think I'm in love," she murmured between groans.

"What happened?"

"He tried to rape me in his Mini. Of course he didn't. I pretended to faint and then he was so sweet, he even did up my bra and helped me to the door, and kept on asking if I was all right."

"How far did you go?"

"Far enough," she replied mysteriously, "far enough." And with that she fell into a deep sleep, snoring loudly, with all her clothes on.

I managed to get her shoes and dress off, but she was too heavy for me to get her properly undressed, so I pulled some covers over her and left her to her snores.

So much for my exciting news about Steve Scott. It would have to keep until morning.

"Don't look so nervous. I'm not going to eat you." Those were Steve Scott's opening words as I stood at his front door.

I must admit to being nervous. After all he is a star and although he's not conventionally good-looking, he's sort of exciting with his long wild hair and very bright blue staring eyes.

"Come in then, don't stand there with your mouth hanging open."

I shut my mouth quickly. Honestly, I must say he is rather rude. My stomach was fluttering. Madelaine and I discussed my date when she blearily opened her eyes this morning.

"Whatever you do you must sleep with him," she had announced dramatically. "It's so dull being a virgin, and it would be simply marvelous for you to be able to say your first man was Steve Scott. Yes, you simply must."

"What's new?" he asked.

"Er—nothing," I replied.

"You're a funny little thing," he said. "How come you were with the big bad Tony the other night?"

"He works for Daddy," I stuttered, "er—what I mean is my father sort of owns Hobo." I wished I hadn't said that. I sounded like some awful little rich girl.

"Who's Daddy then?"

I didn't want to start boasting about Daddy. "Nobody special, just a—er—er—businessman."

"Oh," said Steve, studying me with those bright eyes of his. "What do you do then? Model or actress?"

"Neither. I'm a secretary." That should stop any ideas he might have about me being rich.

"Great! Want to do some typing for me?"

"Yes—if you like."

He laughed. "I'm kidding. You know I think you're for real, a baby innocent."

"I'm eighteen," I lied.

"You're ancient," he replied, still laughing. "Where have you been?"

"I've been at school in Switzerland."

He took my arm. "You know, for an eighteen-year-old bird you certainly manage to come across like fourteen."

I was furious and pulled my arm away, but he gripped it again and said, "Hey, I'm not knocking it. I like it. You don't know how unusual it is. Are you a virgin?"

I blushed.

"You are!" he said laughing. "I bet you are."

Oh, how I wished I had never come. How could he ask me questions like that?

"Let's go and get some food," he said. "I want to hear all about Daddy and Switzerland and why you're still a virgin at your advanced age."

He had a big old-fashioned Bentley, brightly polished. Everyone stared at us as we drove along.

Fortunately, once we reached the restaurant he was descended upon by various friends, and didn't have a chance to question me during dinner. I think by the time we reached the coffee stage ten people had joined us and I was relieved. Actually, he terrified me.

He drank an awful lot, and the language at our table was incredible. I couldn't wait to get away. Perhaps I could just sneak off to the loo and not come back.

"Hey, listen everyone," Steve suddenly said loudly. "This girl's a virgin!" And he clapped his hand down on my shoulder and everyone stared at me.

Oh, floor, please open up and swallow me!

"That's nice for you, Stevie," one of the girls said. "Makes a change," she giggled.

I blushed beet-red. "I think you're an absolute shit," I hissed at him, "please take me home."

"It's nothing to be ashamed of," he said surprised. "You're probably the only eighteen-year-old virgin in England—maybe even Europe!"

I gulped my coffee down, burning my tongue, and was just deciding to get up and leave when who should walk in but Michael, *my* Michael, with that girl he had danced with all night at Hobo. She looked quite ridiculous in a silver tunic outfit.

She came over to say hello to Steve, and Michael walked behind her, saw me and looked amazed.

"Hello, Michael," I waved gaily, my burning

tongue agony, wishing Steve would put his arm around me *now*.

"Hello, Alex," Michael returned my greeting. I could see he was impressed.

"See you later at Hobo," Suki said to Steve, and she and Michael went off to sit at a nearby table for two. What now?

After a while, Steve said "Well what do you want to do—my pad? Hobo? Or there's a party on somewhere."

"I think I'd like to go to Hobo," I said, hoping that Michael would follow shortly.

"Let's go then." He got up and, without even saying good-bye to anyone, we left.

In his car he lit a cigarette and offered it to me.

"No, thank you, I don't smoke."

"That's all right, take a drag, it will put you in good shape."

I gingerly puffed on the cigarette. It had a funny taste and smelled vile.

"There you go, little girl, you're turning on nicely."

"I really don't want any more," I said politely and handed it back to him.

We sat in the car silently while he finished the cigarette.

I know I'm in love with Michael. Here I am sitting next to Steve Scott and *all* I can think of is Michael.

"All right, let's go," Steve said, more to himself than to me. "Let us go out into the night and make it, little baby girl."

Hobo wasn't very crowded. "I like getting here early," Steve said. "You can feel it build up that way."

Soon we were joined by some of the people who had been with us at the restaurant, and others. I was determined not to get drunk, so I stuck to Coca-Cola. I had decided that whatever Maddy said I wasn't going to bed with him. I couldn't even bear the thought of him seeing me without my clothes on. Honestly, the whole thing was going to be embarrassing enough without someone like him.

I watched the entrance, waiting for Michael, which of course was the only reason I was here.

"Come on, let's dance," said Steve. "You *can* dance, can't you?"

"Of course I can!"

On the dance floor after a few minutes he said, "I thought you said you could dance."

"I don't know why you wanted to take me out," I said angrily. "You've just been rude to me all night."

"Oh, come off it, little Miss Virgin, I'm only kidding you. Can't you take a joke?"

"I am *not* a virgin, and I *can't* take your so-called jokes." With that I went and sat down, surprising even myself.

He followed me, laughing. "Them there's fighting words, little girl. Want another Coke or shall we go back to my place and see who's right?"

"Another Coca-Cola please."

At last Suki and Michael came in. She headed straight for Steve. "Carolyn's downstairs," she hissed.

"Oh, shit," he said quickly. "She's supposed to be working tonight. Great!" He turned to me. "See the trouble you're just about to get me in."

"Why, what have I done?"

"Carolyn's my girl, she'll go mad if she sees me with another bird. Look, go over and sit with Suki. I'll see if I can get rid of her."

"But—"

"Go with Suki."

Honestly!

Suki giggled. "Carolyn will scratch your eyes out. Come and sit with us."

So to my complete embarrassment I had to go and sit with Michael and Suki.

Michael said, "What's going on?" and Suki explained.

He wagged a finger at me. "You're certainly getting around in your first week in London."

Michael had his arm around Suki's waist and he kept on giving her little squeezes.

Where was Steve? I didn't want to sit here playing gooseberry to the man I loved.

"Oh, look!" Suki suddenly said. "There's Jan and John, I must go and see them." And she dashed off.

Michael said, "You must be off your bloody stick to be getting involved with the crowd you're with. Haven't you any sense?"

I flushed. "It's none of your business," I replied, absolutely furious.

"Thank God it isn't. Only I hope you don't plan to introduce my sister to your motley friends."

We sat in angry silence until Michael suddenly got up and said, "Tell Suki I'll be back in a minute. I'm going to get some fresh air." Then he just left me sitting there alone. He was insufferable! I would show him I wasn't the stupid little girl he seems to think I am.

# 18

# TONY

On the plane back to good old Blighty I made several important decisions.

1) Get out of Hobo and into something else where I wasn't gripped tightly by the balls by a sex-mad nympho.
2) Tell Alex how I feel about her (I do love her), and give up other girls.
3) Save some money, if possible, in case I should decide on marriage.

My mind was made up that a place called Tony's would be fantastic. I had a lot of friends, and between them I could raise enough money —I didn't need one big backer. The new place would knock Hobo right out. Make it very exclusive. I could picture it now.

First thing tomorrow I'll be out searching for a suitable location. I think I can swing the whole thing for about ten thousand pounds. Now that shouldn't be too hard to raise. If I can only get five people to come up with two thousand each. Sammy must have a couple of grand stashed away, and Hal would be able to find it, and Franklin could talk to his old man. It was all going to work out great.

We landed about midnight and I decided to get a cab straight to the club. I had only one suitcase.

What a trip! I'd hardly even had time to take a pee before I was on the plane home again! Still it was good to be back. I would wait until morning to phone Alexandra. She was probably deep in the land of Nod. Poor little kid having to work at some lousy nine to five job. Maybe one of these days I'll marry her and then she can spend her time looking after me. Oh, boy! Mustn't think about her like that, I can feel myself getting horny. I think the high altitude affects me!

I took them all by surprise at the club. Flowers was chatting to his girl friend at reception—the son-of-a-bitch. He jumped up like he had a candle under his ass when he saw me. Franco was nowhere in sight. Inside a waiter was playing the records and I couldn't see another waiter in the room.

I stormed into the kitchen where it was like an Italian wedding. Franco and the girl cashier were dancing—dancing yet! And the other waiters were slouched around watching. I can't leave the lousy place for a minute.

"Come on everyone," I screamed, "what the fuck's going on here?"

"Meester Blake!" Franco reeled like a startled rabbit. "Meester Blake—we wasn't expecting you."

"Yeah, I can see that. Get back into the room, you lazy slobs. Let's have a little action here, get some drinks moving."

The waiters milled around in panic and confusion while Franco suddenly started screaming at them in Italian. The cashier slinked back behind her desk.

Franco got rid of all the waiters and turned to me crestfallen, "Meester Blake I . . ."

"Yeah, yeah, I know Franco, you weren't expecting me."

I went back inside. Flowers was at his stand, waiters were rushing around looking busy. We were back to normal.

I went over to the regulars' table. Sammy was there, his arm around a horrific little black-eyed teeny bopper. "Tony baby, whatcha doin' back? What happened? Good to see you, boy."

"Yeah," I replied. "Have a drink, Sammy. I'm going to do the rounds, see you in a minute."

I tell you Hobo knocks spots off all those New York joints. It's got what I call classy flash—excitement—call if what you like, it's got it.

I bought a drink here, a drink there, shook a lot of hands, kissed a lot of faces, pinched a few bottoms. Then wowee—pow! Alexandra sitting there as calm as you like. Pretty, she was very pretty, like a gorgeous cultured rose among a lot of dandelions.

*What the bloody hell was she doing here?*

I shook her hand trying to keep cool. She smiled at me. She looked tired. She was with Ring-a-ding Suki and that schmucky student type. I sat down.

"Tell us about New York," Suki asked. Was she with the student or was Alex?

"How do you feel?" I asked my lovely Alex.

"Fine," she said brightly. "You certainly had a short trip."

"Come on darlin'—all fixed," Steve Scott appeared. "Hey, Tony, you back already?"

"Yeah, baby, I'm back." We shook hands.

"Well, come on then," he said to Suki (I thought), but Alex got up.

I watched, shocked, as he took her by the hand and pulled her off to another table.

My Alex with that randy little pop-singer—*my* Alex—*impossible*. There must be some mistake.

"What's she doing with him?" I asked the clown-faced Suki.

She shrugged. "I don't know. I guess he's on another kick—you know, educated Miss Prim-and-Proper, for a change."

"You should be so bloody lucky as to be even a tenth as educated as she is," I said burning. "What is she—prim and proper because she doesn't screw on sight?"

"What's the matter Tony, I only said . . ."

"I don't give a good goddamn what you said, Suki. You're not fit to sit at the same table with her." God I was so angry, I got up and stormed over to Steve and his table of cronies.

"Tony, sit down, have a drink. Tell us about the New York scene."

I could have smashed his stupid face in. "Alex, I want to talk to you," I said trying to appear casual.

"Yes, Tony?" She questioned me with her wide brown eyes.

"Leave her alone," Steve said loudly. "She's mine tonight. Anybody having her is gonna be me. Get it?"

"You're talking to a lady," I said grimly. "And if you don't mind I'd like to speak to her."

Alex got up quickly, she was blushing. I took her out on the terrace and held her very gently by the shoulders.

"Look," I said quietly. "You can tell me to mind my own business, but a girl like you shouldn't be out with a shitbag like Steve Scott."

She brushed her hair back with her hand. "He is rather awful," she admitted, much to my relief.

"Tell him good-bye then. I'll take you home."

"I can't do that. I mean he took me to dinner and everything. I can't be rude."

"Listen, sweetheart, that animal doesn't even know what rude is."

"It's nice of you to be so concerned, but honestly I can manage."

I couldn't stop myself, I grabbed her tightly and kissed her. I pressed my mouth against her lips hard. Her mouth was dry and refused to open, but I pushed my tongue between her teeth and forced her to let me in. I put a hand on her breast and felt its warmth and roundness through her dress.

She struggled and pushed me away. Her cheeks were flushed. "Honestly!" she exclaimed. "I thought you were warning me about Steve."

"Can I see you tomorrow?" Young schmuck asking for a date.

"I'm sorry Tony, I'm busy." She smoothed her dress and looked at me in a funny way, "I'd better get back inside."

"Yeah," I was destroyed. "I guess you'd better."

I felt like I'd been kicked in the stomach. First of all I was hot as hell after kissing her and feeling her fantastic body. Secondly, I knew

I wasn't about to let frigging Steve Scott take her home.

I followed her inside. She sat down beside Steve and he whispered something to her. Bastard! I was going to fix him. I went over to Suki who was busy feeling her boyfriend under the table. God, Massey was well rid of this freak.

"Who did Alexandra come here with?" I asked.

She was mad at me. "I don't know."

I exerted a bit of the famous Blake charm. "Come on, Suki sweetheart, don't be so touchy."

"She came with Steve—and then Carolyn arrived downstairs looking for him—Well, he must have gotten rid of her because that's when he came back and took Miss Goody-Two-Shoes off again. Why are you so interested anyway?"

I shrugged. "She's only a kid, I'm keeping an eye on her."

"Oooh!" Suki the freak shrieked with laughter. "Sir Galahad Blake!"

Michael butted in. "I expect she can look after herself."

I glared. Who asked for his two-cents' worth?

Anyway I had a plan. I went downstairs to the office and dialed Steve's home. As I thought, Carolyn answered. She had been sent home to wait. I disguised my voice (I could have been a wild actor). "Your boy friend's at Hobo making it with another girl" Then I hung up, went upstairs and waited.

Fifteen minutes later Carolyn came storming in, her wild red hair flowing, her eyes mean and narrow.

Steve didn't even see her coming. She gave him a whack across the face that made me wince. "You lousy son of a bitch," she screamed. "What the *fuck* is going on here? Give me some story about you had to show the head of Gloom Records around. Some fucking head." She paused and glared at Alex who seemed cool and collected. "It might interest you to know," she continued, "that this is my fucking husband you're sitting next to. We got married last week and I wasn't supposed to tell anyone because it might upset his fucking fans. So fuck off."

Steve practically slid under the table. What a scene! But Carolyn wasn't finished yet. "I'm three months pregnant too—so stick that up your jumper, you little cow!"

Alexandra had gone visibly pale in the dim of the club. She stood up, "I'm so sorry," she said quietly, "I didn't know," and with that she made for the exit.

She certainly had class, lots and lots of class.

I caught up with her outside. She was crying. I wanted to wrap her up in my arms and carry her somewhere safe. Silently I handed her my handkerchief and she blew her nose.

I called a cab and we got in. I gave the driver my address. This time I wasn't letting her escape. She didn't say anything until the cab reached my place, and then we went through the same old discussion.

"Oh, Tony, it's simply much too late. I must get home."

"Just one quick brandy, you need it."

"I hate brandy."

"Well a coffee then."

"It will keep me awake, please take me home."

The cab driver sat there, his ugly hawk face listening to every word.

"Look, just five minutes, we'll have a quick coffee, a talk and then I promise I'll take you right home."

She sighed, "All right."

I paid the cab and he winked and muttered, "Enjoy the quick coffee, guy." Lousy, dirty old man.

My flat smelled horrible. All the windows had been closed, and something had gone bad in the refrigerator. I let some air in and stuck the kettle on. It was a horrible little pad, I had to move.

Alexandra sat on the sofa and I put on an Astrud Gilberto album. Now that I had her here I didn't know what to do with her.

"This is a nice flat," she said in her best polite voice. "Have you lived here long?"

"A few months, it's too small. I want to move, get somewhere nicer."

We lapsed into silence until the whistle of the kettle boiling. Coffee was a mistake, I should have given her a drink, got her more relaxed.

"How about an Irish coffee?" I asked.

"I've never had that."

Not that I had any cream or brown sugar or any of that jazz, but I could put a slug of whiskey in it, better than plain coffee. "You'll love it."

Astrud was singing "The Shadow of Your Smile." If I had been with any other bird by this time we would have been stripped and hard at it.

"Did you have a nice time in America?" she asked.

"Yeah great." I finished the coffees and handed one to her. It tasted good—personally I don't think you need all that sugar and cream shit.

"You know, Alex, I've got a lot of things to tell you."

She sipped her coffee and stared at a picture of me taken the opening night of Hobo.

"Do you want to go to bed with me Tony?" she said politely, as if asking what time the next bus home was.

I was stunned. I practically spilled my coffee. "What?" I stuttered like an idiot.

She was blushing now and biting her lower lip. "Well *do* you?"

This wasn't exactly the way I had the whole thing planned. I had figured on telling her how I felt, maybe kissing and cuddling her for a while. "Well, yes, of course I do," I said lamely. She had really caught me off guard.

"All right then," she said clamly.

We sat and stared at each other for a bit, and I noticed her hand was shaking as she drank the coffee.

I went to her, took the cup out of her hand and kissed her. This time her lips parted and she gave me a little sigh.

I ran my hands around her body, feeling her squirm under my touch. She was wearing a brown woolen dress, high-necked with small buttons down the back. I started to undo them.

"Can we go into the bedroom?" she asked. "Perhaps I can go in first."

"Yeah, O.K." She had me so excited I didn't know where I was at.

"I'll call you when I'm ready."

She trotted off and left me in a state of shock. Wowee—I had thought she was a little baby innocent. I still loved her though, in spite of the fact that she had obviously—well—been around.

I wondered should I strip? I wished there was time to take a bath, I felt hot and sweaty from the plane trip.

"I'm ready, Tony," a little voice called. "Please don't turn the light on."

She was in my bed, covers up to her chin.

I took my clothes off clumsily, throwing them on the floor. I kept my shorts on and jumped into bed beside her.

She had velvet skin, I wear to God her skin was actual velvet. I could only see her faintly in the darkened room. She had drawn the curtains and wouldn't let me pull the covers off her.

I felt her slowly. Her breasts were very high and full, her waist narrow and her hips curved out, all covered with this wild velvet skin. She lay on her back, her body tense, her hands gripping the covers.

"Relax, baby," I whispered. "Take it easy, enjoy it."

Her body hair was sparse and silky like a fine down. She tightened her thighs when she felt my hand there.

I rolled on top of her and forced the covers out of her grip. She was shivering. I stood up over her and took my shorts off. She shut her eyes and I came back on top of her and worked to get her legs apart.

"Tony, I'm a virgin," she said suddenly after a short silent struggle during which I couldn't shift her legs open.

I felt myself go down like a punctured balloon.

She opened her eyes quickly. "You don't mind do you?"

Mind? Mind! I was delighted. Only it put another aspect on everything. She was a virgin, and she wanted to go to bed with me, which could only mean that she must love me.

"You silly kid, of course I don't mind, I think that's wonderful, perfect."

"Oh, good," I felt her relax.

I rolled off her and gathered her in my arms, and held her.

"You see I don't know what I have to do, I don't know how not to have a baby or anything. It's—it's first time I've ever seen a naked man."

Well, they say if you wait long enough everything comes your way. I felt like a giant! A king!

We lay there for a bit. I was perfectly content just holding her beautiful body. I shut my eyes. I was a bit exhausted from the plane trip and everything.

"Tony, is everything all right? You're not disappointed or anything?"

I opened my eyes quickly. Wow—I was so comfortable and happy that I must have dropped off to sleep for a second.

She had escaped from my arms, and was kneeling on the bed holding a sheet in front of her.

"Of *course* it is, baby. Come back here."

"I just mean—well, if you are disappointed and you don't want to, well—I quite understand."

"You're kidding!" I pulled the sheet away from her and she quickly lay down. I kissed her face and stroked her hair and felt her unbelievably perfect breasts. She started to make little soft noises like a kitten.

I had this funny sort of feeling. Christ! I loved this girl so much. It wasn't even sex. I wasn't so sure that I *wanted* to make love to her. She was so pure and innocent, and maybe she should stay that way.

But she wanted me. She wanted to belong to me. She smelled so sweet, like summer flowers.

I was on top of her and showing her what to do. And she was gasping and biting her lower lip and staring at me with those wide brown innocent eyes.

Oh, God! I pulled out just in time. It was fantastic! Then she rolled away from me and lay on her stomach.

She was mine.

# 19

# FONTAINE

It is such a relief to be rid of the stud. I have learned a little lesson—never take people out of their natural surroundings. My God, look at the zoo, all those poor animals locked up in cages neurotic as hell.

In London in charge of Hobo Tony is a man. Here he is nothing.

I spent a very entertaining afternoon with Alan. I think we are two of a kind. He *did* bring his imagination, and what an imagination! On the pretense of working on a scene for his new book he made me dress up in his clothes, and him in mine! Oh, my, it was hilarious! He even came equipped with a long fall of hair and makeup. A latent faggot, of course, but why should I care as long as it's only latent. I must say he has a lot of possibilities. He told me some absolutely shocking stories about himself and Salamanda Smith. Très risqué! I shall look at the vapid blonde movie queen with new eyes.

Benjamin has arrived and is showering, cleaning his teeth, and gargling. Benjamin is immaculate. Whenever we make love he showers first and after, an infuriating habit, although very hygienic. He changes his underwear and socks twice a day, sometimes three times. As a businessman Benjamin is a genius. But as a husband he is a bore!

Benjamin and I have very little to say to each other. Social gossip doesn't interest him, and financial and business talk drives me to distraction. His children bore me to tears, and he hates discussing my clothes. Actually we are very rarely alone together, perhaps if we were, things would be different.

Once he asked me if I would have a child. I told him that at his age it was a ridiculous idea.

Maybe I should have said yes, but really I wouldn't know what to do with a child. I must say I am quite happy with my life the way it is. I really have everything.

It's so exciting finding new studs and watching their progress. Tony is a prime example—

from a waiter to my lover to—well, what exactly is he? A host I suppose one could call him.

There comes a time in every relationship when a man's body is not enough. I think I have reached that time with Tony. I think he must go. I'll throw him to all the little dollies who may not want him when he's no longer at Hobo.

I must remember to get Benjamin to arrange to have him fired when we get back.

Of course what I really need is a *rich* stud, with all the things that Benjamin has. Then I could divorce Benjamin and *really* be happy.

I don't think I've ever come across one, they just don't seem to exist. All the men with *real* money and position are old and fat, like Benjamin. Poor old Benjamin. Although at times he's not so bad.

"Did you have a nice shower, darling?"

"Yes, very nice. Is my secretary here yet?"

"I don't know, I'll buzz Adamo. I've arranged dinner with Sarah and Alan. He's Sarah's latest husband, a writer, I'm sure you'll like him."

"You know I can't stand Sarah."

"Darling," I went to him and started to pull off his bath towel which was tied around his middle.

He turned away, "Not now, Fontaine. My secretary should be here."

Well, well! Independent Benjamin, after any

separation he was usually rarin' to go. Deliberately I stepped out of my negligee and stretched. "I think I'll have a bath while you're with dear old Miss Clerk. Do you think I'm getting too fat?"

I knew there wasn't an ounce of fat on my entire body. I knew the sight of my body excited Benjamin.

"No, you're not getting fat." His eyes flicked over me, and then abruptly he turned away for the second time.

Was he getting senile at last?

I rang Adamo on the intercom. "Is the secretary here?"

"Yes, madam."

Benjamin was busy getting dressed. "She's here. You will be finished by six, won't you? I promised the Sidwells we would drop by for a drink."

He nodded. I stretched my naked body, blew him a kiss, and went off into the bathroom.

After all if the poor fellow can't get it up, well what can one do?

# 20

# TONY

I can remember when I was a kid seeing all those wild Hollywood movies where there would be some kind of insane love scene, and then the hero (usually Gene Kelly) would say good night to his girl and rush off into the street singing and dancing up a storm.

Well that's exactly what I feel like doing now. Man, I feel like Gene Kelly ten times larger than life.

What if I burst into song and dance in the middle of the King's Road? I'd probably get nicked for being drunk!

I took my little Alexandra home in a cab. She was very quiet, after, very lovable, very shy. In fact, she didn't say a word. She dressed in the bathroom while I snatched a quick kip, then she shook me awake and said please could she go home.

I didn't know what to say to her, I was so sort of knocked out by it all. So we both sat quietly in the cab, and then I dropped her off and let the cab go, and here I am in Chelsea. It's three A.M. and now I'm wide awake, starving, and feeling great.

I picked up another taxi and rode over to Hobo. They never learn—this time there was nobody out front.

I raged inside, grabbed a frightened Franco and said, "Where the hell is Tina?"

"Meester Blake—we wasn't expecting you back."

"Yeah, baby, you're not telling me anything new."

"I think Tina no feel good, she go home early."

"Great Franco—great. So if you let her go home why not put someone else out front!"

"Of course I deed, Meester Blake. Frederico is there."

"Frederico ain't there."

Franco looked shocked. "I keel that Frederico, I told 'im 'undred times to stay out front."

I felt too good to argue any more. I just had to be there, that was all. Franco was fine when I was around.

Flowers was playing Lou Rawls. The place had that nice relaxed atmosphere at the end of a good night, there were about thirty people left in the room.

Sammy was still sitting with his juvenile wonder. He grabbed me. "Where you been? You missed all the excitement. It's a good job I was 'ere, I straightened things out a bit."

"What happened?"

"That Carolyn's a mad bird. She started picking up everything in sight and throwing it at Steve, and 'e's trying to 'ide under the table, and the f-ing and blinding that was going on is nobody's business! So anyway I grabbed a hold of 'er and then she starts to cry and 'e goes running out of the club and then what do you know, the bleedin' newspapers arrive—some joker must 'ave phoned 'em. What a scene!"

I shrugged. I wasn't sorry I'd missed it all, because if I had stayed I'd probably have smashed that half-assed pop singer to pieces.

Sammy's bird sat gloomily in the corner chewing on her thumb. "Can we go?" she whined.

"In a minute, don't be so anxious. I'm going to give it to you," Sammy replied, winking at me and mouthing—"a raver!"

Sammy was still chasing scrubbers. Why didn't he look around for a nice decent girl.

"Hey, Sammy, while I was in New York I was thinking."

"Yee Gods—'e's thinking yet!"

"No, Sammy, seriously. I've got this great idea for opening a new place."

"A new place? Whatcha want to do that for? What's wrong with 'ere?"

"Well, you know, Sammy, I'm the last one to ever see any bread out of this place, it's making a bomb and I see about tuppence."

"Yeah? Well, you're a schmuck, aren't you? Whatcha want to make yourself a lousy deal for?"

"Because I wasn't in a position to make any deal when this joint opened. Anyway—who knew it was going to take off like it did."

"Yeah, well—why dontcha get 'em to pay you some more. You work 'ard enough—*when* you're 'ere, that is."

"Why let them put *more* money in their pockets. This place is *me*—without me they would be finished in a couple of weeks."

"Hold on, boy, you mean a lot to the place, but it still managed very nicely while you were in New York."

"Aw, come on, Sammy, let's go," said the whiny-voiced scrubber. "I'm fed up with sitting here all night."

"Yeah, you go, Sammy, I'll talk to you tomorrow." I could see that I wasn't going to get much out of him.

"Meester Blake." Franco was at my elbow. "There ees Meester Ian Thaine outside with a party of ten, they want to come in, but we cannot serve any drinks now and 'ee is screaming 'bout that."

"O.K., Franco, I'll handle it."

Ian Thaine was a pain in the neck. He had made a fortune in so-called "swinging London" gear—clothes, souvenirs, old uniforms, posters. He had Thaine Shops everywhere, and he made Sammy look like one of the aristocracy. He was about my age, thin and weedy looking, out to better himself socially, but never making it. I knew he hated me, because he saw me chatting to all comers—film stars, Lords, politicians. It killed him. He wanted to be someone. In fact, rumor had it that he hired a permanent press agent to try and get his name in the gossip columns alongside the elite. I suppose he was worth a couple of million at least. He was usually with a motley crowd.

Tonight it was a couple of last season's debs, three members of a scruffy pop group, a once glamorous actress with her nineteen-year-old "manager," a bit-part actor, and two wide-eyed teeny boppers obviously culled from the streets of Piccadilly.

"Ian m'boy," I gave him the brotherly, firm, sincere handshake.

"Tony," he sneered at me, "is that right we can't get a pissing drink?"

"Sorry, Ian, that's right, got to think of our license."

"Balls to your license," he said peevishly. "We want drinks."

I smiled pleasantly. "You'll just have to go somewhere else then."

Ian bit on his lower lip. "Oh all right, we'll suffer with Coca-Cola. I can see I'm going to have to open a place of my own in this town before I can get a drink."

Bingo! Lights flashed. Ian Thaine. Why hadn't I thought of him before?

"Come on, Ian," I put my arm around his shoulder, "I'll buy you all Coca-Colas myself."

My mind was working quickly. Ian was perfect for the setup I had in mind. He would jerk off at the thought of owning a successful joint. All I needed was a little sweet talk. He had the money, plenty of it. We could go fifty-fifty. He to put up all the money, me to put up myself.

"Hey, Ian," I said, "I've been thinking . . ."

I chatted him and he responded like a baby. I'd hardly ever given him the time of day before, because he was an obnoxious son of a bitch, but talking to him I realized just how much he wanted to be liked.

After an exhausting hour of costs and profits and all that jazz, we shook hands.

"It's a deal," Ian said.

Beautiful! He would put up all the money. I would do everything else and get a salary plus forty-nine per cent. I struggled for fifty, but Ian wasn't budging on that.

"We'll call it Ian's," he said.

"Yeah," I muttered. We could argue about that later.

It was all too good to be true. It was late and the waiters were looking mutinous. Ian and party were the only customers left. One of the debs came and plonked herself on Ian's knee. He slid his hand up her skirt. The aged actress was in a tight clinch with her young manager. Nobody looked like budging.

I stood up, "I think it's bedtime."

Ian stood up, the ex-deb sliding in a furious heap on the floor. "Yes, let's go." Ian was now my friend.

To the waiters' relief the whole party got itself together, and we all left.

Downstairs the three pop singers piled into a Ford with the two teeny boppers and roared off. The actress, her manager and the bit-part actor got into a taxi. The two ex-debs and Ian and I were left. He was driving a white Lincoln Continental with gold fixtures and maroon upholstery.

"Where's your car?" he asked me.

"Er—in the garage being fixed."

"I'll drop you then."

"No that's O.K., Ian. I can take a cab."

"I said I'll drop you." He took me to one side. "Besides I want you to take Diana with you. You'll like her." He whispered a speciality that she was expert at.

"Look, Ian, I don't want . . ."

But he ignored me. I climbed in the back of the car with Diana. She was horsy-faced, tall and skinny. I couldn't have fancied her on the best of nights.

"Where to?" Ian asked.

I told him. How the hell was I going to get out of this?

I mean he obviously thought he was doing me a big favor. The best thing to do was play it by ear.

He dropped me off and Diana clambered out with me.

"See you at my office at three then," Ian said. "Have a good time."

Shit! He drove off and Diana and I stood there. "Where do you live?" I asked her when the car was out of sight.

"With Ian," she replied, slightly surprised. "Why?"

It looked like I was lumbered. Why was I such a jerk? Why hadn't I taken Ian to the side and explained. I suppose because I wanted a deal, and if accepting one of his tatty girls was going to please him, well I guess I would just have to accept her.

"Come on," I said wearily.

Please forgive me, my wonderful Alexandra, but I'm doing it for us.

# 21

# FONTAINE

Benjamin is not himself. Surly, bad-tempered, and positively rude to Sarah and Alan. I am absolutely furious. I've never seen him like this. Of course I know he's a monster in business, but with me he has always been placid and polite, and never verbally attacked my friends, which he did quite viciously last night, calling poor Alan "a lily-livered poor man's Tennessee Williams." Well, I mean, really! I didn't know he'd ever read anything of Alan's.

Sarah was livid. I have rarely seen her angry, but last night her eyes were flashing and the words practically spitting from her lips. Needless to say we all parted outside Le Club simply dreadful friends. I haven't spoken to Benjamin since. How dare he think that he can insult me and my friends!

Alan says he knows about us. What nonsense! How can he possibly know. I'm always discreet.

On top of everything else we have the added thrill of beastly little Ben junior joining us tonight. Alexandra is bad enough, looking down her nose at me all night, but Ben junior is impossible. Mutual hate abounds.

What I would actually like to do is go back to London. I expect I am missed there.

I have decided to wait a few weeks before having Benjamin fire Tony. After all, he is different in London and I may as well make use of him until I find another London stud. I must say I feel quite nostalgic about Vanessa and Hobo and all the little intrigues.

Oh, God, I suppose I shall have to make peace with Benjamin. Why the hell I should make peace I don't know, and I *do* want to buy that sable coat today and it *is* twelve thousand dollars. I'll put on my white mink over nothing and go and wake him.

Benjamin, of course, is already up and at his office. It is noon and he always rises at seven.

Adamo remained impassive at the sight of me wandering around in my coat. Dear Adamo, the perfect servant.

Benjamin wouldn't appreciate me turning up at his office in my mink and nothing else. The erotic secret of being naked underneath is very exciting. But of course Benjamin is much too staid to enjoy it.

I phoned Sarah. "Darling, I'm so sorry, I'm just too upset for words."

Sarah's voice was acid. "I'm sorry for *you*, sweetie, *you're* married to him."

"That's all right darling. He's full of remorse today. I'm just off to get a new sable."

"They're more chic in Paris this year."

Sarah was a bitch, but I could out-bitch anyone. "Why don't you buy Alan one?"

She laughed coldly, "You're so amusing, Fontaine, maybe I shall."

We said our good-byes, and I phoned Benjamin at his office.

"Yes, what is it, I'm busy."

Oh, my God, he was impossible. It crossed my mind to forget the coat and let him beg my forgiveness. But a sable coat is worth a slight effort.

"You're not still angry?"

"What is it, Fontaine, I'm busy and can't discuss things now."

"Well, darling, I need some money."

"Talk to my secretary, she'll send over what you need."

"Twenty thousand."

There was a pause. "Twenty thousand dollars?"

"Yes, darling, I've seen a gorgeous sable coat, and I have to get a few other bits and pieces."

"But I just bought you the white mink."

"I know, darling, but I *need* a new sable."

"No, Fontaine, we'll talk about it later."

"What do you mean, *no* Fontaine?" I was shaking with fury.

"Good-bye." He hung up on me.

I phoned back at once. "Mr. Khaled is in conference, and can't be disturbed," an embarrassed secretary said.

"But this is Mrs. Khaled."

"I'm sorry, Mrs. Khaled, he said I wasn't to interrupt him for anyone."

I slammed the receiver down. How dare he! How dare he! He would pay a lot more than a sable coat for this.

# 22

## TONY

I think I'm a right bastard. What I should have done was told Ian Thaine to take his messy little ex-deb home with him and screw the fact that it might louse up our deal. If our deal depended on me knocking off one of his birds, then to hell with it—who needed it?

I did. Who even knew he was going to come up with the money anyway? So far it was all conversation.

I really felt bad. Diana had gone, I had to force her to go. She was disgusting. And I was disgusting too, laying back and letting her slobber all over me. Well, at least I hadn't touched *her*.

I have definitely decided I'm going to marry

my little Alex. It's a big decision, I know, but I love her. I truly love her. I think I would kill any bastard that tried to touch her.

The whole situation is very dodgy. I've got to get away from Fontaine and Hobo. Christ, if Alex ever found out about me and Fontaine it would be all over. She's a girl of principles, so sweet and kind, and that body! Wowee! I've never seen such a gorgeous body, and I've seen some bodies in my time. Firm velvet skin, so shy, and a virgin. I can hardly believe it, and she's mine, all mine.

I think what I'm going to do is get up; dress, and maybe take Alex to lunch. Of course, I don't have her office number. I should have asked her last night, but maybe her girl friend is home.

I dialed their flat, but there was no reply. Shit! I couldn't even remember the name of the firm she worked for. It's twelve o'clock, which means I've got to wait five or six hours before she gets home.

I had to meet with Ian Thaine at three, that would pass the afternoon. Maybe Sammy would fancy a bit of lunch.

I couldn't track Sammy down, but I found Hal and Franklin in our favorite coffee bar, a nice little place where you could sit all day and watch the tourists go by.

Hal said, "Listen, baby, I've got a beautiful deal going. You remember Mamie? Well, her old man invested in this film company in Rome before he died, and now the company's going bust and she's putting up a lot more bread and I'm taking over. We're leaving for Rome tomorrow. Beautiful, huh? If you're a good boy I'll put you in a movie, you're pretty enough!"

Hal came up with a deal like this every so often, but something always fucked it up, usually him.

"That's great, Hal, you're going to be a big man."

"Baby, I'm always a big man." His smoky eyes surveyed two American ladies struggling with their mink stoles. He was always on the lookout. "How was my town?"

"Great, Hal, great, I had a ball."

"Yeah, one of these days I'll go back. I'm waiting for my bookie to die! Got to be a success in that city, baby, otherwise you're nowhere—but nothing."

My favorite waitress came scurrying over. "Morning, Mr. Blake. Same as usual?"

"Yes, pretty. Make sure the eggs are nice and firm."

She dimpled a smile at me. "I see your club made headlines today."

"What?"

Hal said, "Yeah, baby, didn't you see it? A load of shit about Steve Scott."

"No." I patted my waitress on the bottom. It felt like she had nothing on under the flimsy blue skirt and white apron. "Be a darling and grab me the papers."

"I'll try, Mr. Blake. We're awfully busy just now."

She returned in two minutes flat with three morning papers. I scanned them quickly. Steve Scott was on the front page of all of them. The headlines screamed about his secret marriage. I read the first article.

"Steve Scott (23) disclosed at London discotheque Hobo last night his secret marriage to actress and dancer Carolyn England (23) sometime last week. Steve Scott found fame two years ago when his record 'Laurie Baby' shot to the top of the charts. Since then his records have stayed consistently in the Top Ten. He has just finished recording his own weekly TV Show and is due to start work shortly on his first film *Mud*. Miss England has appeared countless times on your TV screens and was last year voted 'The girl with the longest legs on TV.' The news broke when Miss England surprised her husband at Hobo, where he was enjoying a quiet evening of fun with Alexandra, eighteen-year-old daughter of billionaire Benjamin Al Khaled. The new Mrs. Scott also announced that they are expecting an addition to the family. The Steve Scott Fan Club hung a black flag from its windows early this morning. Steve Scott has no comment on this surprise marriage."

There was a big picture of Carolyn in a black fishnet catsuit leering sexily, and a small picture of Steve having his shirt ripped off by a band of fans.

I was really furious. Where the hell had they got their information about Alexandra? Why should her name be brought up? Lousy newspapers. They all carried more or less the same story.

My poor baby Alex would be upset if she saw it. Well, it would teach her a lesson for going out with the randy little bastard in the first place. I attacked my eggs.

"Hello, mind if I sit here?"

It was Suki, dressed for the day in a thigh-length Indian shift and a fringed jacket.

Franklin said, "Where's your sister? You promised to fix me up."

"Oh, yes, sorry, I've been busy. I forgot about it. I'll talk to her."

I don't understand Franklin. He has every opportunity to score with all the birds at the club, but he never makes a move. Now he's hanging his hopes on Suki's sister.

"If you promised him, do it," I said. "Get your sister for tonight."

"She might be busy," Suki replied producing her compact and studying her freaky face. "Anyone seen Massey lately?"

Under all the piles of makeup she was probably quite pretty.

"What do you want to know about Massey for? You've got your little student now," I said.

"I just wondered if anyone had seen Massey, that's all," she replied defensively. "I thought he might be here today."

I finished my eggs and ordered some cheese cake. Eating is one of my favorite pastimes, but I never get fat, I stay in great shape. Twenty-five push-ups a day. My stomach's hard as a rock.

Just then who should walk in but Massey. Cool as ever in a white suit and brown polo-neck sweater. He's a great-looking guy.

"Tony." He clapped me on the shoulder. "Good to have you back. Hello Suki—Franklin—Hal." He sat down at our table.

Suki snapped her compact shut and put it away. "Mass, can I come back?" she asked.

"No," he said quite gently, "no, baby, you stick with your little white boy."

Her clown eyes filled with tears. "Oh, come on, Mass, let me back."

"I said no, Suki." And he turned to talk to me about New York.

Suki sat there a few minutes, then with two big tears hovering in her eyes she got up and left.

I ate her open cheese sandwich, which she hadn't touched.

"She thinks she can just come walking back to me when she gets a little bored with her sweet little white boy," Massey said grimly. "Well, she can just sweat it out."

I think Massey was actually jealous.

I hung around until it was time to meet with Ian Thaine, then I walked the short distance to his office.

He sat on a black leather throne in front of a huge antique desk in a red room hung with pictures of himself. His opening words were, "I told you you'd get a good job done, didn't I? Those little convent-educated cunts are the ones." His face was thin and evil and his eyes thin, yellow slits.

"Yeah, well thanks, Ian."

"It's nothing."

He then proceeded to give me a full sex summary of the three females he had living with him, including Diana. Then he unlocked a desk drawer and produced a stack of Polaroid pictures of them in various stages of undress. They became obscene. I felt sick to my stomach.

"I took them all," he said proudly. "Sometimes I have special parties. Next time I'll see you're invited."

Here was a man after Fontaine's heart! Was I climbing from the frying pan to the fire? What about getting down to business?

I flicked through the rest of the Polaroids and said, "Very nice Ian. Now what about contracts and things?"

"Contracts?" he said. "What's the matter, don't you trust me?"

"Of course I trust you, but if I'm going to start knocking myself out looking for locations I want to be sure everything's cool—you know, have it all down in black and white. Of course as soon as we find something I'll leave Hobo."

One thing I was sure of. I wasn't going to be Tony Schmuck again. If I had to get involved with this slimy bastard it was all going to be legal, so that when he wanted me to attend any of his parties I could safely say no without getting chucked out. Fontaine unwittingly had taught me to be smart.

"All right," Ian said. "I'll have an agreement drawn up. Meanwhile start looking. What about Mrs. Khaled?"

I looked at him in surprise. How did he know about me and Fontaine?

"What about her?" I said suspiciously.

"Shall I mention her in the agreement?"

"What for?" Now I was really surprised.

"She's your—er—partner, isn't she? She'll be in it with us, won't she?"

I was speechless.

Ian carried on. "I'd like to meet her. When can I meet her?"

Well, this was charming. When had I ever mentioned Fontaine?

"She's in New York," I said vaguely.

"Now there's a beautiful woman," Ian said admiringly, locking his Polaroids away.

I stood up. "O.K., Ian. I'll wait to hear from you then."

"Yes, I'll have my solicitor draw something up. Shouldn't take long."

"Fine, I'll start looking."

We shook hands. I didn't trust him, but as long as he thinks Fontaine is involved he'll probaby come up with an agreement and the money. I don't know why he thinks she's my partner, but if it keeps him sweet, let him think it. Why disillusion the poor schmuck before the time came?

I couldn't wait for my little Alex to come home from her office. I wondered what she would want to do tonight. I wasn't going to take her on any wild outings, just a nice quiet dinner somewhere small, and a serious talk about us. Then she was going home to bed early. My darling must get some sleep. I figured I would drop by a few real estate agents to pass the rest of the afternoon. May as well start the ball rolling.

# 23

## ALEXANDRA

I don't think I've ever been so embarrassed in my life! Mr. McLaughton summoned me into his office. I was a half-hour late this morning, and I suppose this is it.

He was a huge man with bushy eyebrows from under which peered watery red eyes. "Sit down, Alexandra," he boomed. "You don't mind me calling you Alexandra, do you?" and he chuckled.

I sat nervously. Father was right. I should have taken a job with one of his friends.

"Well, well, well," Mr. McLaughton said, suddenly lapsing into a fit of coughing. "So we have a celebrity in our midst."

"A celebrity, sir?" I questioned dimly.

"You are Benjamin Al Khaled's daughter are you not?"

How on earth had they found out?

"Yes, sir."

"You should have told us. Why so secretive?"

I blushed. "I don't know, sir."

Honestly, what was I expected to do? Come marching in for the job announcing to all and sundry that my father was Benjamin Khaled?

"I think we can give you a better position than you have," Mr. McLaughton said beaming. "I think we can bring you into my office as a junior personal assistant, at an extra five pounds a week. Not that the money matters to you, I'm sure."

I didn't want to be brought into his office as junior personal assistant at an extra five pounds a week just because they knew who my father was.

"Thank you sir," I muttered. I'm weak, I hate to cause scenes. I would have to phone or get Maddy to phone and say I couldn't work there any more.

"My two daughters think Steve Scott is marvelous, you'll have to get them his autograph."

I looked at him in astonishment. "Steve Scott . . ." I stammered.

He picked up a newspaper from his desk and waved it at me, "Pretty girl he married," he said. "Is she a friend of yours too?"

I took the newspaper from him and read it quickly. The whole thing became clear. That's how they knew about me.

"I haven't seen this," I mumbled.

"Well, don't forget about the autographs. You can take the rest of the week off if you like, start your new job on Monday, heh? Perhaps I can meet your father one night, have a little chat about his talented daughter." He chuckled again.

"Yes, sir. Thank you, sir." I fled.

By three o'clock I was home. Madelaine was out. I phoned my mother. Apparently she hadn't seen the newspapers because she didn't mention anything about the whole mess.

"You are bringing some friends this weekend, aren't you?" she said.

"Yes, maybe."

"All right, jolly good, darling. See you tomorrow then."

Madelaine came in shortly after, laden with packages. "I've been shopping," she announced. "Got myself some great gear. What on earth are you doing home? And have you seen the papers today?"

"Yes. I've seen them. Why do you think I'm home? As soon as my boss found out who I was it was all 'Oh we'll give you a raise' and 'Take the afternoon off.' Isn't that phony? I don't think I'll go back."

We talked while she unwrapped her parcels and tried everything on.

Maddy had discovered via Jonathan that Suki had been sleeping at their flat, and that even worse she had moved lots of her things in.

"Jonathan's absolutely livid!" Maddy said. "It's only a tiny flat and her things are everywhere. He says Micahel is dotty about her. Sorry, but I'm sure it won't last. I say, when are you seeing Tony again?"

"I don't know, never I hope."

"Oh, Alex, he's gorgeous, awfully good-looking. He's your lover anyway, you'll have to see him."

"No I won't."

We had discussed my losing my virginity from seven A.M. when Maddy finally woke, to eight-thirty, when I had rushed to the office. Maddy had asked a thousand questions. Did it hurt? Did I love him? Was he enormous? Did I scream? I couldn't really remember any details. I suppose he did have a nice body. Of course I didn't love him, I loved Michael. Michael, Michael, Michael, that's all I could think of. As if my thinking of him produced some magic power the phone rang, and it was him.

"Alex? You want to have dinner tonight?"

"Dinner?" I was staggered.

"Yes, I want to talk to you sensibly."

"O.K., fine."

"I'll pick you up about eight."

"All right."

I was delighted. I told Maddy and she gave a wise nod.

At six o'clock who should phone but Tony. "Well beautiful, how do you feel?"

What on earth did he want?

"Fine, thank you," I said.

"About the papers today, look, I'm sorry, it's horrible for you."

"It's not *your* fault."

"Yeah—well I wish I could have stopped it. Anyway what time shall I fetch you?"

"Fetch me?" I racked my brains to think if I had made any arrangement with him for tonight, and I was sure I hadn't.

"How about eight o'clock? We'll just have dinner and then I'll bring you straight home."

"Look, Tony, I'm awfully sorry but I am already going out."

There was a long pause, then he said, "You're kidding?"

"No, I've had this arranged for ages."

There was another long pause and then he said, "Well, break it."

"Break what?"

"Your date. I'll fetch you at eight."

"Tony, I can't, it's . . ."

His voice was suddenly very angry. "Who are you seeing that's so bloody important?"

I hated people being angry with me. "I'm sorry, Tony, it's—it's family, I just can't get out of it."

"Oh, Alex, Alex. What are you doing to me?"

"I'm not doing anything to you."

"Are you angry with me about last night, is that it?"

"Honestly I'm not angry. I'd love to see you, but it's just not possible tonight."

"All right little girl. How about later?"

"I'm not sure, I don't know—"

"I'll call you at eleven, if you're not tired I'll come over for an hour before going to the club. How's that?"

"Terrific." I breathed a sigh of relief to get him off the phone without a nasty scene.

I borrowed Maddy's crochet dress and Michael actually gave a whistle when he saw me. "You *are* growing up," he commented.

He took me to a little restaurant, very dark and cozy, and lectured me solidly about how I was mixing with bad company, and if I didn't watch it I would get into trouble, and that all these people I was always with smoked drugs and things. Well, I *knew* that.

"I feel responsible for you," he said. "You can't come straight out of school and turn into the town swinger. What did your parents say about the papers today?"

"Nothing," I muttered. I was sulky and

disappointed. I thought he had wanted to have dinner with me, but he just wanted to tell me what a silly little girl I was.

"Anyway, what about you and that funny girl?" I finally said, unable to keep quiet any longer. "What do your parents think of *you* living with her!"

"I'm not eighteen years old," he said grimly. "I'm only trying to help you, Alex, you're only a kid."

I decided I hated him yet again.

I was home by ten-thirty, having bid a cold good-bye to Michael immediately we finished dinner. Tony phoned promptly at eleven.

I would show Michael. I invited Tony to spend the weekend in the country. Michael had called Tony common and loud. Well, let's see what he thought about this! If this doesn't make him jealous, I don't know what would.

# 24

## TONY

You drift through life from day to day and everything's cool. Life is good, things swing along nicely, plenty of birds, friends, food, enough bread to gamble a little, eat out every night. Beautiful!

Of course I always wanted to do a bit better, get my own joint. But I knew I didn't have to push, it would all happen. I could just relax and enjoy life. It was such a blast to have names I'd only read about treat me like their long lost brother, to have any number of fantastic birds available.

Then along comes Miss Alexandra Khaled, shining auburn hair, big brown eyes, knockout body, young, innocent, classy, sweet, shy, kind. And I fall—*POW!!*—in love.

It means an immediate change in my life. I need plenty more bread, not for gambling, or eating out. But I need to make a home. I have to have something to offer her. Right now I wish I'd listened to Sadie and saved some money.

She looks at me with those big trusting eyes and I melt. I never in my life felt this way before. I feel I must look after her, protect her from the world.

When she said she couldn't see me tonight I was destroyed. My whole day had hinged around seeing her in the evening. I was angry and jealous and sick to my stomach. But she explained so nicely, so sweetly.

Oh, boy, I never thought I'd get caught like this. I've known a lot of women and I thought as far as they were concerned I had it licked. Screw 'em and leave 'em wanting more. Never failed. But now I was caught in that well-known trap. When she said she couldn't see me it was a feeling of physical pain.

Of course I had to marry her. This was it. Put her in a little flat, give her a few kids. I wonder if she can cook?

I spent a miserable evening with Sammy and his whiny-voiced scrubber from the night before. We ate at a steak house and I'll swear she was giving him a quick one under the table. She sucked her thumb between mouthfuls of food, and wiped her nose with the back of her hand. Charming!

Eventually she went to the loo and Sammy said, "What's the matter with you—what are you dragging for?"

I shrugged. "Nothing. I'm fine." I wasn't about to tell *him* what the matter was.

"So, what do you think of my bird? Still at school, isn't she a little darlin'?"

"You won't be happy until you get caught, schmuck. She's under age."

"Who's going to catch me then? She says 'er parents never ask any questions. She can come and go when she wants."

"Sammy," I shook my head sadly, "what do you want it for?"

"You're kidding, aren't you?"

She came back. She looked all of fifteen in her wisp of a dress and long pattern-stockinged legs.

Eleven o'clock came very slowly. I tried to stay cool and phoned Alex.

She was adorable. "I'm in bed, Tony, I've been home ages."

"I'll come over and read you a bedtime story."

Oh, God, I was coming out with lines I didn't even believe

"I'm just going to sleep, but I'll tell you what, would you like to come to the country for the weekend?"

"When?" I asked stupidly.

"I thought tomorrow afternoon, and we could come back Sunday evening."

"Yeah, that would be great."

Screw the club, it would just have to manage without me over the weekend. A whole three days with my Alex. Couldn't be better.

"Shall we take the train?" she said. "Or do you want to drive? It's only an hour's trip."

I didn't think Sammy would see fit to part with his E-type over the weekend so I said, "We'll take the train."

"There's a four o'clock from King's Cross. Mother will meet us at the other end."

I had forgotten about dear old Mummy. That sort of put a damper on things. What if Mummy told Daddy and Daddy told Fontaine? Oh, well, I'd soon be away from Hobo.

"Yeah, that's perfect. I'll pick you up around three."

"What happened to you?" Sammy asked. "You look like you found gold."

"Yeah," I laughed, "let's go to the club."

It was going to be one of those nights, jamming up early, plenty of faces, Franco on his toes, Flowers playing Wilson Pickett. Hal, Franklin, and Massey were in already, Massey with a zoftig blonde, Franklin alone as usual, and Hal stoned, celebrating his last night of freedom before Rome and Mamie.

I socialized a bit. It was too soon to put out the word I would be opening on my own, but it was as well to spread my charm heavy. I must remember to pinch the members' list and get it copied.

"The Twang" came in with a film group, pouty lips, mane of tangled orange hair; she had got over her temper with me. She gave me a hug and a kiss, her tits hanging out of a black velvet dress. She wasn't a bad kid, we had had quite a lot of fun. She was certainly built.

"Guess what, Tonee baby," she squeaked, "I'm starring in *Mud* with Steve Scott. Isn't that fabulous?"

"Yeah, great." I felt full of goodness toward the world.

"What did *she* have to say?" Franklin asked when I sat down.

"She says she's starring with Steve Scott in *Mud*."

"Huh!" exclaimed Franklin. "Candy Cook is the lead, she's probably got a bit part." He still hadn't recovered from his encounter with "The Twang."

"Franklin," I said seriously, "what are we going to do about you?"

"What do you mean?"

"I mean you getting laid, that's what I mean. What are you saving it up for? Wow—if I was your age with your connections I'd be having a ball."

"I just haven't met the right girl."

"Shit, man, by this time *any* girl would be the right one. You can't jerk off all your life, you know. I'll tell you what, I feel so good tonight I'm going to personally find you a girl."

Franklin lapsed into silence and I went and had a Scotch with one of The Must, just back from a record-breaking concert in Paris.

There's something about a Scotch and Coke I like. It's a good long drink with a hidden punch. I must have had about six or seven when I went to take a piss and realized I was well and truly loaded. I usually just get a little buzz on when I'm working, but tonight—like *POW!* It had really hit me.

I was sweating hot, having been dancing with Molly Mandy, who's a wild dancer. She had wandered in on her own and sat at our table. I had this vague idea of fixing her up with Franklin, but God Almighty, she'd eat him alive! Maybe that's what the kid needed.

Out of the blue I found myself dancing with "The Twang."

"Ooh! Tonee this is fun," she squealed. "You never used to dance with me when we were together."

Funky Street. Flowers freaking out at his stand. "The Twang" shaking her boobies at me. Man, I was gone. Flowers grinning broadly. Jumpin' Jack Flash. Sweat pouring off me. Hal having a screaming match with Franco. Everyone laughing. Everyone having a ball. Sammy doing it with his schoolgirl. Tramp. Why did Otis Redding have to get it in a lousy plane crash? Flowers in mourning for weeks, more so than for Martin Luther King. You're lookin' good. "The Twang" falling out of her dress, giggling, tossing orange hair around. Suddenly she changed into Molly Mandy, and I said, "Do me a favor and ball Franklin."

The music was getting slow, slower. Who was I dancing with? Carla Cassini, beautiful Italian movie star. She smelled fantastic, but ruined the whole thing with hairy armpits. "You ees beeg man, yes?" I left my heart in San Francisco. Was that Massey with Suki? And the zoftig blonde dancing with Hal? Hal never danced, but he was swinging tonight. Who wasn't!

"My producer—he 'ave to return Roma for one day only, so I came see you tonight. Good idea, yes?" She was an armful of woman. What about Alex? Would one more time be wrong? Who can I turn to? She moulded her body into mind, rubbing a leg between my thighs. Christ, she caught me in the balls and it hurt. "We must be careful," she muttered. "I am followed—'ee always has me followed." Can't take my eyes off you. She churned her body into mine, keeping perfect time to the music.

"I stay at 102 Marlofield, a leetle 'ouse. You come in one 'alf hour to the back window—I arrange everything."

Shit, man! Franco and the Italian waiters were hovering at the edge of the dance floor trying to get a better look.

"I go now," she said abruptly, and left me standing there.

It never rains but it pours. I sat down.

Molly Mandy was hard at work whispering in Franklin's ear. He looked a bit stunned. Man, the room was turning. "The Twang" appeared. "How about tonight for old time's sake?" she whispered in my ear, wriggling her tongue about in there at the same time.

Molly Mandy gave me a wink across the table. Massey and Suki came and sat down. A short fat guy I didn't know came over to "The Twang" and clamped a chubby hand on her shoulder. He had a cigar clamped between his teeth, "You gonna stay with this jerk all night?"

"Oh, Chucky, sorry. I'll be right back."

"You'd better," he said.

"Who's that?" I asked.

"That's Chuck Van Marless—junior," she said. "The producer. I'd better get back."

"So who's keeping you?"

She gave me a sad look. "You're such a bastard, Tonee."

Her voice got on my nerves. She wriggled

her way back to Chucky, junior, and the group she was with.

I love Alexandra.

What number Marlofield Square did Carla say? After all I wasn't married—yet.

Franklin and Molly Mandy suddenly got up. "We're going," she announced with a big smile, flashing her gold fillings. Franklin studied the ground in embarrassment. At last, at last!

"What about my sister?" Suki said.

"Where *is* your frigging sister?" I asked.

"Well, she's here—somewhere. She saw some friends when we came in, but she'll be over soon and she thinks Franklin is her date."

"Listen, baby," Massey said, "I do not believe she's too anxious. You've been here an hour already and where is she?"

Suki shrugged. "Let's dance."

They went off, happy to be together again.

I couldn't remember the goddamn number—a hundred and something—102, that was it. I was going. After all a movie star is a movie star and what Alex didn't know wasn't going to hurt her. It certainly doesn't mean I don't love her. Anyway it's a well-known fact that fellows need it more than birds. So what about Fontaine?

I grabbed a taxi and, remembering Carla's warning, had him drop me off in the Square, where I wandered around looking for 102. It was impossible work finding the numbers, and pissing with rain, but I went from house to house peering at doors with my trusty cigarette lighter. Oh, God, what one wouldn't do for a star!

I found it. I hoped she had some Scotch and Coke, I needed it. I pushed my way past clumps of trees to the back and started trying the windows. I was soaking.

Suddenly a light shone in my eyes and a loud voice said, "I'd stay just where you are if I were you." And then a big copper loomed into view. "What do you think you're doing then?' he inquired politely. One thing about our policemen, they've got lovely manners.

So there I stood wet through and just approaching a hangover in West London Central Police Station. Charming! The bloody copper had never heard of Carla Cassini, nor had the couple who lived in 102 Marlofield Square. Too late I realized it should have been Marlofield Street, but the sweet arm of the law didn't want to know about checking my story. I imagined Carla waiting for me in a clinging black slip, the sort of thing she wore in most of her movies.

I was in a right mess now. What a scene! After long arguments they finally sent someone around to check my story at 102 Marlofield Street, and Carla, the bitch, denied she'd even heard of me! So then more arguments until I finally got them to phone Hobo and Franco and Sammy came rushing over and identified me. Franco confirmed that Miss Carla Cassini had been in the club that night, and had been dancing with me. So they finally believed me and let me go.

Shit, man! Sammy was laughing so much that tears were rolling down his cheeks.

"I can just picture the scene," he said, "you trying to get in a window what a 'ard on, and the copper pouncing down on you!"

Oh, very funny. Very funny indeed.

Franco was trying to look grave and concerned wedged in the back of Sammy's E-type, but I knew as soon as we got back to the club the story was going to be all over.

"Now I don't want this spread around," I said grimly.

"Meester Blake?" Franco exclaimed in horror. "I cut off my right arm eef I say anything."

Lying son of a bitch!

# 25

## FONTAINE

I sat and planned my revenge. It was about time Benjamin was taught a lesson. God Almighty, he was treating me like a wife!

I dressed, went out, and bought the sable coat anyhow. Benjamin's credit was good, they knew who I was. "Send the bill to my husband's office," I said. "He always likes me to pick my own Christmas presents."

That would teach dear old Benjamin to say no to me. Doesn't the old fool realize how lucky he is to have a wife like me?

Tonight, when he expects me to entertain his beastly son, I shall make mincemeat of them both. Benjamin can't expect to treat me this way and get away with it. First of all I intend to return to London tomorrow, with or without Benjamin. I will show him who calls the tune in *our* marriage. My God, if he thinks he can push me around the way he used to treat his dreary first wife he can think again.

I put on a white lace Courrèges cat-suit. Roger came by and fixed my hair in a devastating style, then Adamo made me a champagne cocktail, and I awaited my darling husband's return.

He puffed in promptly at six, followed by Ben junior, who peered at me though owl-like glasses. "Hello, Benjamin darling," I purred coldly, ignoring the son. "So sweet of you to call me back."

"Did you see young Ben," Benjamin said pointedly.

"Yes, I saw young Ben," I replied in a sing-song voice.

"Fontaine pull yourself together. We'll talk about it later."

"There's nothing to talk about. Oh, by the way, I bought the coat. It's in the bedroom—it's absolutely divine. Thank you, darling."

His face sagged, but he was loath to argue in front of his precious son. He turned brightly to Ben junior, "Well, now, what restaurant would you like to go to?"

"Anywhere, sir," Ben junior replied, studying the floor in embarrassment at being caught in the middle of an argument.

"What about you?" Benjamin turned to me, desperately trying to keep the proceedings bright.

"I don't think I'll come." I savored his look of annoyance. "I have a headache."

There was a short delicious silence, then Benjamin said, "Make yourself comfortable, Ben, have a drink, look at the magazines. Fontaine, why don't you come into the bedroom and show me your coat while I shower."

Oh, I see. He was going to forgive me for buying the coat if I came out to din-din like a good girl and was nice to dreary, boring son.

I was right.

"Fontaine, don't be a bitch."

"A bitch?"

"You know what I mean."

"What?"

"The boy is sensitive. Don't hurt him; make him at ease."

"And how about *me*? I'm sensitive too, especially when some goddamn little secretary won't even put me through to you on the goddamn phone."

"You must understand . . ."

"So must you. I don't expect to be treated like this."

"You have the coat now, at least you can be civil."

"Yes—I have the coat *only* because I ignored you and got it anyway."

"Oh, Fontaine, yes you have your coat now. I know my money and what it can buy you is the only reason you married me. You don't love me and I think I've finally realized it."

"Save me the sob story, please."

"Please, Fontaine, be friends now for the boy."

"He's not a boy, Benjamin, don't baby him. He's probably bored stiff at having dinner with us anyway, and so am I—very bored with the whole thing."

"I'll see you get the rest of the money you want tomorrow morning."

"Oh, all right then, but just remember *never* to treat me in such a way again."

"All right, Fontaine, but please let us have a nice amicable evening."

I hate Benjamin. I hate a man you can tread all over.

His punishment wasn't over yet, he would see. As soon as he comes pawing me, expecting to go to bed with me, he will just have to wait. Just as he had to wait before we were married. Oh, God, I had him mad for it then, and that's just the way it's going to be again. He'll have to beg for it. On his knees. Poor old bastard.

# 26

## TONY

Charming! Hauled down to the police station like a common criminal! Sadie would have a thousand fits if she knew. All over some Italian bird that if you want the truth I didn't even fancy! Well not much anyway, I mean if she hadn't've been who she was I certainly wouldn't have gone creeping down to Marlofield Square—street—or wherever it was. Really, I don't fancy anyone except Alex.

It is two o'clock in the afternoon, and I'm shaved and dressed (very casual—white sweater, black slacks, suede jacket). I am wondering what kind of jazz to take with me. A suit in case my darling wants to go out? Pajamas? I don't even have any on account of the fact that I always sleep in the raw—lets the skin breathe, y'know.

In the end I bundled a couple more sweaters and my shaving gear in a bag. After all, a weekend in the country was bound to be slopping about.

I didn't feel too fantastic. Slight touch of a hangover. But I looked good, with some overnight tan I could have just got back from the south of France.

Alex was waiting for me. Very pretty in a green trouser suit, with her hair tumbling around her lovely little face. She had a huge suitcase and said, "I'm taking all my dirty washing home!"

Sweet!

"Do you want some coffee?" she asked.

"I've got a cab waiting."

"Oh, O.K. Maddy won't be a sec."

Maddy? Don't tell me she was coming with us. What a lumber!

She was. Maddy in a mauve trouser suit with a big fat bottom, a John Lennon cap, and a homely face.

I had been looking forward to a nice quiet talk with my Alex, but it was not to be. On the train Maddy kept up a nonstop stream of unintelligent conversation, all about clothes and some schmuck called Jonathan and wasn't Christmas going to be absolutely "super." I gathered from the conversation that Alex was going to spend

Christmas at Madelaine's house. Charming! I would have to talk her out of *that*.

"Mother always goes to St. Moritz for Christmas," Alex remarked to me—*finally* including me in the conversation—"it's so lovely there with the skiing and everything. This will be the first Christmas I haven't gone with her."

"Only another week and I haven't bought *one* present yet," Madelaine exclaimed. "What do *you* want Alex?"

Alex laughed. "Nothing actually. Where are you spending Christmas, Tony?"

Where was I spending Christmas? The Elephant and Asshole, I supposed. "Er, I haven't decided yet."

As a matter of fact Sadie and Sam don't keep Christmas—I mean, nothing special. Usually on Christmas Day I get up late and wander over to the Hilton with whatever bird I happen to be with, and eat their special Christmas lunch. It's very nice. Then I wander home, get into bed and watch TV.

I fell asleep to the sound of the girls' chatter. I would get Alex alone later, I could wait.

"Wake up, we're here!"

I staggered off the train behind the girls, carrying Alex's enormous suitcase, Madelaine's ton-weight overnight bag and my carryall. Tony the porter.

The girls raced off up the platform and I

followed. Alex threw her arms around a fair-haired woman standing beside a station wagon. She smiled at me when I came lumbering up with all the gear.

Alex said, "Mummy I should like to introduce Tony Blake."

She gave me a friendly smile. I could see where Alex got her beautiful brown eyes. Her mother was an attractive woman, a lot better than any of the old birds Hal ever appeared with.

"So glad to meet you, Mr. Blake. You'll have to excuse my daughter leaving you to carry everything, she has absolutely no manners."

We all laughed. I liked Mummy.

We reached the house, I was shown around, then left alone in a mahogany-lined guest room with an adjoining marble bathroom. What a house! Stables, swimming pool—the lot. Servants darting around everywhere, three cars in the drive. I had imagined poor abandoned Mummy living in a cottage with a daily help. Really I was a bit choked. How could Alex have a billionaire father, a mother that lived like this, and *still* work as a crummy secretary? I couldn't understand it.

A butler came in with my bag. "Shall I unpack for you, sir?" He looked disdainfully down his long thin nose.

Oh, shit, man—if Sammy could see me now!

"No, that's all right," I said airily, thinking of

my two crumpled sweaters and a clean pair of pants with a hole in.

"Are you sure, sir?"

"Yeah, I'm sure." I glared at him, hoping he would go away.

"Can I fetch you a drink, sir?"

Now that was more like it. "Yes, I'll have a Scotch and Coke, plenty of ice."

"Scotch *with* Coca-Cola, Sir?"

"Yeah—*with* Coca-Cola."

"Very good, sir."

Skinny old bastard, didn't know what it was all about stuck down in the country.

I opened my only piece of luggage and wished to hell I'd brought a suit. Alex and Madelaine had deposited me in this room saying gaily, "We're going to change for dinner—see you downstairs at seven." I had nothing to change into except another sweater, and I was saving that for tomorrow. I had an awful feeling that I'd brought the wrong gear. I hadn't even been alone with my baby Alex yet. Where the hell was her bedroom anyway? I'd have to know that for later.

Long thin nose came back with a tiny slug of Scotch in a glass, a full ice bucket and a bottle of Coke.

I down the Scotch in one fell swoop. Then I changed sweaters and went off in search of Alex.

It was a huge bloody house with massive oak

doors everywhere—all closed. I went downstairs and in front of a roaring fire I found Mummy in a blue chiffon cocktail gown, with a red-faced giant of an old chap in a dinner jacket.

"Ah, Mr. Blake," Mummy said. I wished she would cut out the Mr. Blake jazz. "I'd like to introduce you to Doctor Sutton."

I shook hands. Well at least they were going out somewhere the way they were all dolled up.

"Mr. Blake is a friend of Alexandra's from London."

"Oh, yes," said Doctor Sutton. "How nice—yes, London, I shall be going there in three weeks' time. Friend of Alexandra's. Charming girl, just like her mother y'know—charming. Yes—very nice, very nice."

"Would you care for a drink, Mr. Blake?" asked Mummy. I can't bring myself to call her Mrs. Khaled.

"Yeah—I mean, yes, thank you, lovely. Er—I wish you'd call me Tony."

"Certainly." She smiled. She had a smile like Alex, only it was a little worn around the edges.

She summoned long thin nose who smirked knowingly at me and said, "Scotch *with* Coca-Cola, sir."

"Yeah."

"Now that's a funny drink." Doctor Sutton

wasn't one to miss out on a bit of conversation. "Very funny, you drown the taste of the alcohol with the carbonated drink. You may just as well drink plain Coca-Cola."

I wished the old goat would get going, and where was my Alex? As if on cue she came in with Maddy. Both of them wearing quite dressy outfits. It suddenly dawned on me that maybe dressing for dinner meant dressing up for dinner.

Maddy confirmed my suspicions, "Haven't you changed yet, Tony?" she asked, just as old long nose was bringing me my drink.

"Hush, Madelaine," Mummy said. "Mr. Blake doesn't have to change."

"Oh, gosh, Tony," Alex interrupted. "I forgot to tell you we always dress for dinner. I thought you would know . . ." she trailed off lamely. "Please forgive me, why on earth should you."

Yeah. Why on earth should I know. After all I'm only a lousy ex-waiter. I felt like a downright fool.

"Don't worry about it, Mr. Blake. You look quite respectable as you are," said Mummy.

So I stood there with egg on my face while they all inspected my black and white striped (at least it was Simpson's) sweater and tight black trousers.

Madelaine stifled a giggle. What she needed was a good stiff kick up her backside.

"Dinner is served, m'Lady." Old long thin

nose was back. I thought scenes like this only existed in the movies.

We all trooped into the dining room, Alex holding my arm and whispering, "Sorry!"

The dining room table was loaded with enough silver to sink a ship. It's a good job I was once a waiter—otherwise I'd never have known which knives and forks and jazz to use.

Dinner was a gas: Doctor Sutton entertaining us with a story about a patient of his with a terminal disease; Mummy telling us about how she was coming up to town for the January sales and what she was going to buy; and Alex and Madelaine occasionally giggling together.

I was well and truly fed up. After dinner, which dragged on, there was coffee in the study, then everyone started yawning and Mummy said, "We'd better all have an early night if we're to go riding in the morning."

I tried to catch Alex's eye, but she was in a huddle with her girl friend as usual.

"You *do* ride, don't you Mr. Blake?" asked Mummy. I'd kill her if she didn't stop calling me Mr. Blake.

I felt like saying, "Yeah, baby, I ride, but not the way you have in mind!" Instead I said, "No."

"What a pity. But you can have a nice rest and we shall be back by lunchtime."

Oh, very jolly.

Everyone said good night to everyone else and the girls and I started upstairs while Mummy saw the Doctor out.

"Where's your room?" I hissed at Alex.

"Oh!" she looked flustered. "Maddy's in with me."

Charming! "Then you come to my room."

"Tony I *can't*, not here."

I took her sweet little hand and squeezed it, "I just want to talk to you, only talk, I promise."

My body was talking already; I was as hard as a rock.

"I'll try."

I gave her a kiss on the cheek as Madelaine stood and stared. "Make it soon."

She nodded. "If I can." And then she was off with her girl friend.

What a lousy situation. I mean what a drag this whole thing is. I was really up tight. I looked at my watch. Only nine-thirty. I haven't been to bed at nine-thirty since I was ten!

I went to my room. No television, no radio, no telephone. Someone had turned the bed down and unpacked my bag. Well what the hell—I didn't care what some thin-nosed butler thought of me.

I lay on the bed and smoked a cigarette—then another one, then another.

This was ridiculous, nearly half an hour and no Alex.

I couldn't bear the thought that she wasn't going to come. My body was in a nervous sweat already. I would give her another five minutes—ten minutes—fifteen minutes. Goddamn it! Nearly an hour and where was she?

I went out into the passage. No sign of life, just a dim light burning. Like an idiot I had no idea where her room was. I peered through the keyhole of the door next to mine, it was darkness; then the next keyhole, it was a john; then the next, a cupboard. I was making great progress.

The passage curved round a corner, and there was a door with light showing under it. I bent down to peer through the keyhole and jerked back with astonishment. Naughty old Mummy. She was spread out on the bed, yards of blue chiffon around her waist, legs high in the air, and crouched above her was dear old Doctor Sutton. Mummy was a right raver.

I couldn't help smiling. What a scene! Doctor Sutton still had most of his clothes on—couldn't be too comfortable!

Well, well, well. I dragged myself away from the keyhole—I was a doer not a watcher.

Now I felt horny. Where was Alex?

I set out down the other end of the passage and started the keyhole routine again. Her room was in the same position as her mother's, but *she* wasn't, she was lying asleep in a divan bed with a small table separating her from Madelaine, also asleep.

I looked at her for a while. I felt like a thief. She was breathing softly with the covers pulled up to her neck and her hair spread out on the pillow. I had such a feeling of *love*. Keeping a wary eye on Madelaine who was giving out with a few snores, I gently pulled the covers off Alex. She was wearing a white frilly nightgown. She sighed and turned onto her back.

I was eating her up with my eyes. My body was choking to hold her. I put my hand onto her breast so soft and still, her eyelids fluttered and I quickly took my hand away.

She opened her eyes. "Tony!"

"Sssh." I didn't want the girl friend awake. "What happened to you?"

She looked a bit sheepish. "I *meant* to come and talk to you but I fell asleep."

Very flattering—I mean she really must have the hots for me.

"Well come on," I whispered.

"But it's so late and what about Maddy," she protested. All the same she climbed out of bed and slipped on a pink quilted dressing gown.

I took her hand, "Maddy's fast asleep, and I'll have you back in bed in no time." She didn't realize I meant my bed, of course.

We crept off down the passage to my room, and she curled up in a chair and stared at me with those big brown eyes.

I paced about a bit and turned off all the lights except for a bedside Tiffany.

"What do you want to talk about?" she asked sweetly.

I stood beside her chair and stroked her hair. If I didn't have her soon I was going to explode.

"I'm sorry about dinner," she said, "I should have warned you we always dress—Mummy's a stickler for doing things properly."

Yeah, baby!

"Alex," I said, my voice strangled. I started to undo the buttons of her dressing gown.

She pushed my hands away. "It's a shame you can't ride," she said in a high little voice.

Oh, but I can—I can.

My hands reached her beautiful breasts and I squeezed her nipples. She wriggled around in the chair trying to get away.

"Stay still—relax," I said. I was shaking. I wanted her so badly. I was a fine one to tell her to relax.

I managed to slip her nightie over her head. Her hands flew to cover herself and she started to shiver.

Then I played the strong man and carried her over and plopped her on the middle of the bed. She still had on a pair of white panties and she lay quickly on her stomach so all I could see was her smooth velvet back and her rounded bottom through the panties, and long knockout legs.

I ripped my clothes off. If I wasn't quick I was going to blow the whole setup. I lay on top of her. Oh, man I could have made it all over those sexy legs! But I gathered a little control and pushed myself between the back of her thighs. I stroked her back and pushed my hands under her and grabbed her breasts.

She tried to throw me off. "Please stop it, Tony. I don't want to—*please* "

But when she started to cry, loud sobs, I felt the world's worst heel. This wasn't some bird I was on the make for, this was the wonderful girl I wanted to marry.

"Hey." I got off and cuddled her softly. "Easy little girl. If you don't want to, we won't, no problem."

She got up quickly and put her things on. I took her to the door, kissed her, and she smiled at me and said, "Thank you, Tony. Good night." Then she was gone.

Man, this is really love. If I can give up what I just gave up, I really have it bad. And now I have a problem, and not even a *Playboy* magazine in sight!

# 27

## ALEXANDRA

Maddy woke me in the morning by pummeling my back until I was forced to open my eyes. I yawned. "What time is it?"

"It's seven, and where *were* you last night? I got up to go to the loo and you were gone. Did the devastating Tony drag you off to his room and ravish your girlish body?"

"Oh, Maddy, shut up, you sound like some woman's magazine."

"Did he screw you then?"

"Maddy!"

I went off to the bathroom before she bagged it, and took a cold bath.

I wanted to discuss it with Maddy, but it was just too personal.

Maddy was all huffy when I finished in the bathroom.

"You've become very secretive," she remarked coldly.

We had breakfast of scrambled eggs and bacon; then we set off riding. I had my own horse—Pinto.

I felt guilty about last night, guilty about upsetting Maddy, and guilty about everything in general.

We were riding through the woods and approaching a stream when suddenly Pinto reared up and I came tumbling off.

Mummy and Maddy had already crossed the stream, but they stopped and turned back.

I felt all right, nothing broken, but when I tried to stand my left leg gave way and I felt an awful pain.

"I think you've got a bad sprain." Mummy said.

"Oh, Alex!" Maddy lamented.

They piled me back onto Pinto who was now standing quietly, and back to the house we all went.

Mummy sent for Doctor Sutton who came immediately.

It was a sprain, and a nasty one.

"Off your feet for five or six days at least," Doctor Sutton pronounced.

"Poor Alex," Maddy wailed.

Mummy was very businesslike. "Can't be helped. I think there's a two o'clock train to town that Mr. Blake can take. What about you, Madelaine dear? Do you want to stay or will leave too?"

I groaned. I was beginning to feel sick. "I think you had better go back, Maddy. *I'm* not going to be much fun to be around."

"If you're sure, Alex. I'll stay if you like."

"No," I shook my head. Doctor Sutton had given me some pain killer and sleeping pills and I was feeling very drowsy.

"Come along, Madelaine dear," Mummy said. "She'll feel better if she has some sleep."

They went out of the room. My leg throbbed, my head ached, and my eyes soon closed.

# 28

## TONY

Too bloody much! Sitting on another train next to best friend Madelaine, without so much as a last glimpse of my adorable little Alex.

"Rotten luck, isn't it?" Madelaine questioned for the sixth time.

I think she gets some sort of perverted thrill out of seeing me so choked.

"Yeah," I muttered, wishing she would shut up.

"What will you *do* tonight?"

"What I always do on a Saturday night, go to the club."

"You're so lucky. I'm left in the lurch, my boy friend's away and I hate staying in the flat alone."

Tough!

We have five minutes of beautiful silence, then—

"I say, Tony, could I come to the club with you? I'd be ever so good, stay out of your way and everything."

I frowned. Who needed her?

"Well no, Maddy, it would be a real drag. You'd get shoved around all over the joint. Saturday night's a madhouse."

"*Please*, Tony. I don't mind. I'm sure Alex would want you to take me. In fact she did mention something about us sticking together."

Sticking together? What was *that*?

Shit, why had my little darling gone and fallen off her goddamn horse.

"That's settled then?"

Christ! Didn't she ever shut up? The poor guy that ever got lucky would probably have to gag her while he had it off.

"All right." I said reluctantly. I didn't want her carrying tales to Alex about how I wouldn't take her to the club.

She prattled on about God knows what. I was bored by her. King's Cross at last!

"Can I share your taxi, Tony?"

Caught once more.

She talked all the way to Chelsea and left me with "Can you pick me up about eight o'clock?"

Oh, no, definitely no.

"Sorry, Mads, I've got to pop over and visit my mum and dad. If you want to come by the club I'll be there from about twelve."

That should fix her. Her face dropped.

"What a shame. I thought we could have dinner first."

"Sorry, darling, duty calls."

"Oh, Alex will be disappointed when I tell her."

Anyone would think it was Alex I was turning down!

"You know how it is. Maybe I'll see you later."

I hopped back in the cab and muttered to the driver, "Get moving."

"See you later," Madelaine shouted bravely.

She didn't intend to give up, but I doubted if she would come waltzing into the club at midnight. I felt pretty blue. I'd been feeling like a king the night before on account of that whole scene with my darling, but now she was lying injured in bed and they hadn't even let me see her before I left. I had decided to talk to her about our plans, get everything settled over the rest of the weekend. I certainly wouldn't have minded staying at the house while she was in bed, but Mummy had Madelaine and me out of there like a shot out of a gun.

My flat looked worse than ever. I could never expect Alex to move in here, even to start off with. Maybe if we got rid of Madelaine *I* could move in with Alex.

I was thinking of perhaps Caxton Hall for the wedding, do it quickly before anyone could object. I'd have to talk to her about it as soon as I saw her again, and when would that be? With randy old Doctor Sutton in charge, who knew?

Anyway, come Monday morning I am going to be out and looking for new club premises. As long as Alex is away I may as well get *something* settled.

# 29

## FONTAINE

Benjamin and I flew back to London in silence.

Our whole relationship has been based on silence ever since that ghastly evening out with Ben Cretin junior.

When we were coming in to land Benjamin suddenly gripped my arm and said, "I want a divorce, Fontaine."

"You want what?"

He cleared his throat and I studied the network of tiny age lines all over his face.

"I want a divorce," he repeated.

I gazed out of the window completely at a loss. The old fool asking me for a divorce! How ironic. How humiliating. How dare he!

I smiled coolly. "Sorry old boy, but I don't

think I care for that idea." Inwardly I was in a burning rage.

"You have no choice," he said sourly. "I've had you watched." He produced a thick wad of papers from his briefcase. "I know *all* about you and Alan Grant and Tony Blake. I even have photographs."

He handed me a glossy ten by eight of me and Tony on the bed in the New York apartment.

Oh, my God, I looked awful, and Tony so hairy, like a great ape—ugh!

"Where did you get this?" I asked pleasantly.

"Adamo."

"Oh!" That little bastard! I couldn't think properly. I had to see my lawyer immediately.

"There will be two cars meeting us at the airport," Benjamin said. "I have a suite at Claridge's, and you may stay at the house until it's sold."

My head was spinning. What had I done to this old man that he could treat me like this?

"Of course I will make you a reasonable allowance, though I don't have to, and we'll call the sable coat a farewell gift." He stored his evidence back in his briefcase and the wheels of the plane touched gently down.

For some utterly stupid reason my eyes filled

with tears and I said, "But I thought you loved me."

He looked at me seriously, "And I thought you loved me." He unclicked his seat belt and stood up, "Good-bye, Fontaine, good luck."

# 30

## TONY

I had a good sleep. Didn't feel like seeing anybody so went to a movie on my own and arrived at the club early. There was nobody in yet. I sat down and told Franco to have the chef fix me a steak and chips.

Flowers wandered in and sat down beside me. He looked moody and miserable.

"How's it going?" I asked.

He shrugged. "Not good man." He chewed on his fingernails.

"So what's the problem?" I knew it was bound to be a touch, but I wanted to keep him sweet as I had plans for him and Tina in the new joint.

"I need á fast fifty for Tina, she in trouble."

Charming! A touch is a touch, but fifty?

He chewed on his fingernails some more while I did some quick thinking. I wanted them with me when I went, and what better way to guarantee that fact than by having him in my debt. Besides which, I liked Tina, she's a good hard-working kid.

"O.K. I'll get it for you. Monday."

Flowers beamed. "You're great, Tony, I knew we could count on you." He went off to tell Tina the good news.

Fontaine will be furious when I am gone. I don't give Hobo ten days without me. The plan was to set the new place up, have it all ready to go, and then bye-bye Mrs. Khaled.

Where is Mrs. Khaled anyway? Still in New York I hope, enjoying her strange scenes.

The money people started to arrive and were placed carefully out of the way. Flowers put on an early Antonio Carlos Jobim album. One of The Must arrived alone and sat down with me. He was about the most intelligent of the group but always high on acid. We discussed sounds and how the police were always raiding his joint but he was too smart for them—he kept all his gear buried in the garden!

"Where's Lissy?" I asked. Lissy was his flaxen-haired sixteen-year-old freak-out wife.

"She's taking a health bath in Germany."

"Oh." I mean what else do you say to *that*?

Sammy bounced in alone "I've been workin' me bleeding' balls off!" he announced "I'll have a Scotch and Coke."

I got up to greet some faces. A well-known politician and his new wife Who should they be with but mumsy old Vanessa and husband Leonard. She smiled nervously at me. huge tits escaping from purple tulle. Leonard shook my hand, good clean masculine stuff. I had a feeling he couldn't stand me. In this business you get a pretty reliable sixth sense about things like that.

Everybody started to arrive at once. and Franco got busy sorting them all out. There were certain places certain people would sit, and certain places they would not. Franco knew exactly, and he was great at arranging them all

I stayed near the entrance, greeting, kissing cuddling, flattering.

Vanessa came out to the ladies' room and whispered. "Can I talk to you, Tony?"

"Yeah." Why all the hush-hush? We were well out of sight of hubby.

"Have you heard about Benjamin Khaled?"

"Heard what?"

"Apparently, and I know this from a very good source, my hairdresser actually."

"Get on with it," I was impatient.

"Well you must promise not to breathe a word of this to Fontaine. Do you promise?"

'Yeah, I promise." She was impossible.

"Actually he's been seeing another woman, and not just any other woman—Delores! My dear Fontaine will be beside herself with utter rage when she hears. She would never dream Benjamin could stray. Isn't it too too frightful?"

Without tits I would never have looked at Vanessa in the first place, now, even with them, she didn't appeal to me at all. Gossip gives me a pain. I patted Vanessa on her fat bottom and winked. "Don't believe it."

"But it's true! Honestly Tony. Delores goes to the same hairdresser as me and I heard that . . ."

"Still don't believe it."

She pouted. "Nanny takes the children out every day between three and four as before. Why don't you come to see me?"

I shrugged. That scene was definitely over. "Yeah, maybe."

She laughed nervously. "Don't say maybe, say yes."

I was saved by Sammy appearing. " 'Ere, any loose stock around?"

Vanessa gave him a look of distaste and disappeared into the loo.

Sammy chuckled. "You've always got a bird 'anging around you. What you got that I 'aven't?"

One of the good things about Sammy is that you never have to bother to answer him.

The evening roared on. I stayed sober, rejected a few girls and felt pleased with myself. I wasn't going to be unfaithful to my darling Alex. I didn't want to be, and I wasn't going to. There's true love for you.

Just before one Madelaine appeared. "I've had a simply dreadful time getting in," she complained. "I came at twelve and that ghastly foreign girl said you weren't here yet, and she wouldn't even let me in to wait. Then I came back and she *still* said you weren't here, so I waited till she wasn't looking and just came right on it. Really, I do think you should fire her."

She looked lumpy in some sort of crochet dress, and a bit red-faced. Tina had *strict* instructions *never* to let any unaccompanied birds in, especially if they asked for me.

I sat her down next to Sammy who looked her over with some disinterest. I ordered her a Coca-Cola, wasn't getting *her* loaded. Then I did a fast vanish and sat down with a couple of song-writers who had the current hot show in town. Idle chat. Then up to greet an old-time movie star, five feet tall. He looked like a giant on the screen. He was with "The Twang" who was fast becoming everybody's date.

"Tonee babee," she squealed. "You're going to be so proud of me. I'm signed for two new movies. First *Mud* and then a picture with my gentleman friend here." She squeezed old-time movie star's arm and giggled. Her left tit reached his mouth!

I wondered if she'd still be available for me if I wanted her, or did she only put out for a part in a movie now?

"That's wonderful," I said, phony bastard that I am.

"Yes, isn't it though. I'm so thrilled, it's all so wonderful! Have you got a good table for us?"

All of a sudden she was talking to me like a waiter!

"Franco will see to you." I went out front. Tina said shyly, "Thank you, Mr. Blake."

The poor kid looked washed out.

"Why don't you go home, one of the boys can come out here."

"Mr. Blake I'm fine—really."

I felt like taking off early myself.

"Tony!" A shriek from a deep throaty voice. "You old sexy bastard. How *are* you, darling? Still the greatest fuck in town I bet!"

It was Margo Castile, famous sex change . . . lady. I mean *he* was originally a fishmonger or something, but after many operations *she* was a well-known personality around town. Rather exotic, lovely looking, but with this deep butch voice and language like a fishwife. She was with two men, a small beaming Italian and an English actor.

"Tony darling. When are you going to show me what you keep in those sexy tight pants!" She shrieked with laughter. She was always drunk.

"Yes, Tony!" the English actor lisped excitedly. "When are you going to show Margo?"

I smiled weakly. I wasn't ready for *this* group tonight. We all went inside.

"I say, let's have an organized fuck!" Margo shouted. "All those that want to join in hands up!"

"Shut up, you are awful," giggled the actor.

I got them seated at a table and warned them to behave. Margo laughed and patted a pretty blond girl sitting at the next table. "You're sweet," she drawled, "perfectly sweet! Do *you* fuck?"

The girl gasped and turned away. Margo roared.

"Look, if you can't behave," I said, "I'll just have to throw you out." I was always threatening her with that, but it never did any good.

"I promise to be a good girl." She smiled at me. "Promise, promise."

She was a nut, but you couldn't help liking her.

Back at my table, Sammy was chatting Madelaine.

" 'Ere, who is she?" he whispered.

I told him all I knew.

'Not much to look at, but I bet she's a lunatic in bed!"

He was welcome.

I suddenly decided the hell with it. I was going home. The place gave me a goddamn pain. I briefed Franco and quietly left.

Who needed it?

# 31

# FONTAINE

I couldn't believe that Benjamin wanted to divorce me. How could he? After all I had done for him, given him. It was outrageous, and what was I going to do? I wasn't seventeen, I wasn't a girl ready to start her life all over again.

In spite of the early morning I phoned Tony. Of course there was nothing he could do to help, but perhaps I would spend the day with him, indulge myself, take my mind off things. What else was there to do on a Sunday?

He was asleep—well naturally.

"I thought you might like to come over and welcome me back," I said.

His voice was a sleepy blur. " 'Er, I can't, my mother, always see Sadie on a Sunday."

"Really." I hung up. The arrogance of him was incredible! Turning me down for his mother. Why if it wasn't for me he'd still be running for a tip!

Everyone treated me so badly. I am too nice, that's my trouble. I let people use me, only Benjamin isn't going to get away with it. The old bastard can think again if he imagines he can treat *me* like this. I am not his ugly first wife, ready to be quietly discarded like a little white mouse.

Of course the whole thing has come as such a surprise, although I should have realized as soon as he came to New York and wasn't ready to leap straight into bed with me that *something* was amiss.

There must be another woman. A scheming money-grabbing *bitch!* I go hot and cold with sheer and utter anger. *How dare he.*

And as for that Adamo, I shall see he never works anywhere again. How revolting to think of him watching me in bed. Where on earth was he hiding? And Tony, Alan. Were they in on it?

I can't wait to phone my darling friend Vanessa. If there is gossip around she will know of it.

As it was a Sunday I was forced to wait until at least ten to phone her, and then I got Leonard.

"She's still sleeping, Fontaine. We were at your club last night. When did you get back?"

"This morning. How was the club? Anyone interesting?" Leonard then started to tell me a boring story about how Margo Castile had done a striptease down to brief bikini panties.

"Fantastic bosom," he added. "All there, just like a real woman."

"Injections darling, you too could have one like that. Although what you're worrying about bosoms for with your wife's mammoth proportions I don't know."

He laughed, slightly embarrassed. "I'll get Vanessa to phone you when she wakes. I'm sure you two a lot to catch up on."

Did he know something?

I prowled around my house. My beautiful house that was up for sale. Oh, just wait until I get in touch with my solicitor tomorrow.

Vanessa didn't phone until twelve.

"Fontaine, sweetie, how are you? When did you arrive?"

"This morning."

"You must be exhausted!"

"No, I feel wide awake actually. I thought I might come over and catch up on all the gossip. I'm sure there's lots of it."

"I'm still in bed, but I'd adore to see you. Come for lunch. Leonard's out golfing."

"Divine."

I was depending on Vanessa's being able to tell me exactly what was going on.

I was right. She couldn't wait to tell me all about Benjamin and a ghastly scrubber model called Delores.

"Why on earth didn't you phone me in New York?" I demanded. My God, had I known, I would have been in a much stronger position.

"I thought you knew," replied my loyal friend, sloppy in a blue cashmere cardigan with a button missing. "Apparently he's given her a huge emerald and diamond ring, a car and several fur coats."

"How nice." My voice was acid.

"What are you going to do?" Vanessa gushed.

I shook my head slowly. "Divorce the bastard, and take him for every penny he's got."

# 32

## TONY

I have phoned my lovely Alexandra every day. But each time I get old hawk nose the butler or Mummy. Both tell me Alex is fine, making wonderful progress, but can't come to the phone yet. Charming! Today is the last straw. Phoned as usual and was told Miss Khaled had left to spend Christmas with the Newcombes.

It's Christmas Eve, pissing with rain and miserable. I have spent a lousy week searching for a new place. Haven't come up with anything. The club has been a drag, everyone away for Christmas. Even old Sammy hasn't been in.

I miss Alex like mad, in *every* way. It is getting difficult not to take some bird home and bang her purely for physical reasons. Fontaine is back, maybe I should have seen her when she phoned. On top of everything else I have a lousy cold.

I spent hours trying to find the Newcombes in the phone book. Why hadn't I been nicer to Madelaine? Now she was with my Alex somewhere, and I couldn't even phone. Damn! Mind you, Alex should have phoned me or something. But then I remembered she didn't have my number or address. Oh, well, get Christmas over with and then she'd be back, everything was going to be fine.

After Christmas Eve the club shut down the five nights, opening again on the night before New Year's Eve. I got the flu and collapsed in bed during that time. Ate out of cans and spent a really miserable Christmas in a cold sweat and fever.

Sadie came over once with a jar of chicken soup and a lecture about how this was all due to too much sex. Too much sex yet! Ha!

"You live like a pig," she said. "When are you going to settle down, get yourself a decent job. You should see your cousin Leon now living in a big house in Finchley, a lovely wife, baby on the way. When are you going to find yourself a nice girl that you're not ashamed to bring home to your parents?"

I was too sick to tell her about me and Alex, she'd know soon enough. I gave her a hug and a kiss and told her not to worry. "I'll have a surprise for you soon," I said. Dear old Sadie. Her one ambition in life was to see me married so she could have a few grandchildren to cluck over.

A doctor friend of mine came by, gave me a shot and told a few dirty stories. The next day I felt better and got up. I had wasted away five days. Hey, it got me through the holiday season.

I shaved, dressed and phoned Alex, *still* no reply at her Chelsea flat.

I phoned Ian Thaine and he was out. I wanted to get hold of the contract. I was sure to find a property this week.

I went to the club and looked through the reservations for New Year's Eve. The place was going to be a madhouse—booked solid.

When the hell was Alex coming back?

# 33

## ALEXANDRA

"Super to see you," Maddy said, "I have *so* much news."

It was good to be out of bed and about again. My ankle felt fine; and I was looking forward to spending Christmas at Maddy's house.

"Is Michael here yet?" I asked anxiously.

"Coming down tonight, it's all over between him and that model girl, you'll be glad to know."

"Yes, I know. He called me every day. He was absolutely furious that I took Tony down to the house for the weekend. I honestly think he was jealous. But after telling me off he was so nice. I just can't wait to see him. What's it been like in London all alone? How's Jonathan?"

Maddy shrugged, "All right. I say, Alex, I've

met this awful man and I'm simply *mad* about him!"

"Who?"

"Well, after I got back to London Tony insisted I go to Hobo with him. I met this friend of his, quite old, a raging cockney, but *so* funny and frightfully sexy. I just couldn't help myself, I did the most ghastly things with him!"

"Maddy! What about Jonathan?"

"I saw Jonathan one night, but he was so dull. Sammy makes hats and I went to his office one day and he gave me two. Alex, he's Jewish. My mother would have a fit!"

"I can't believe it. Have you actually—well you know . . ."

"Not exactly—everything but though. I think I shall after Christmas. I promised him I would. He's frightfully pleased I'm a virgin. Oh, and Alex I have the most juicy piece of news. Sammy says that Tony and your dearest stepmother are having a violent affair. What do you think of that?"

I felt sick. How could I ever have let him touch me? It was obscene. How awful. He had probably been laughing at me all along. Perhaps he had even told Fontaine all about me. I shuddered.

"Maddy, you're kidding?"

"No, it's quite true. Sammy told me all about it, said it's the only reason Tony is at Hobo.

Ghastly, isn't it? I say, Alex, I thought we might pop down to the shops, get a few last minute things."

I shook my head numbly. "You go, Mads, I've got a headache."

# 34

# FONTAINE

"Mrs. Khaled?"

"Yes."

"My name is Ian Thaine."

"Yes?"

"Er—you do know who I am?"

"No, Mr. Thaine, I do not."

"About the new club, our new club. Tony Blake has told you it's me that's putting up all the money."

"What new club?"

"The new club, the place that's going to take over from Hobo. I thought perhaps you and I should meet since we're going to be partners."

"Mr. Thaine, I don't have the slightest idea what you are talking about, but it sounds interesting, perhaps we *should* meet. Tell me, are you anything to do with Thaine shops?"

"I am Thaine shops."

"How nice. Perhaps you would care to come for tea today, about four. Oh, Mr. Thaine, don't mention anything to Tony Blake about our conversation, let's just sort it out between ourselves first."

# 35

## TONY

New Year's Eve is a drag. They should print little badges with that slogan on and have everyone who feels the same way as me wear one. A poor excuse for a giant booze-up, wreck-up and fuck-up. Of course I wouldn't be here tonight if it wasn't important to keep up contacts—out of sight out of mind as the saying goes. With the new club practically set I had to be in touch with everyone.

The club was festooned with balloons, paper balls, party hats, blowers—the lot.

I got there very early, choked because I had finally got an answer from Alex's Chelsea flat, and Madelaine had informed me that Alex was out and wouldn't be back until late. Out where?

She didn't know. Who with? She didn't know. How was she? Fine. Madelaine Newcombe is an up-tight bitch. I left the club's number and my home number and told her to have Alex phone me the minute she came in. I was going to get some things sorted out fast. In fact I didn't see any reason why we couldn't get married at once, nip into Caxton Hall, and keep it a secret until the new club was all set. Great idea—maybe tomorrow—New Year's Day. It was the best way. Do it, then tell people. That way Fontaine couldn't try and stick her nose in.

Flowers appeared wearing yellow pants, black shirt, and embroidered sheepskin waistcoat.

"Very smart," I said, thinking that some of my bread had ended up on his back.

He put on Sergio Mendes and went into the kitchen for some food. Not a bad idea, there was at least another hour until people would start arriving. I hadn't phoned Sammy, Massey or any of the boys. They were probably at Steve Scott's party. I wouldn't go near the little bastard, although his wife (ha!) had phoned while I was sick and begged me to come.

I had a steak and a couple of Scotches—had to get in some sort of festive mood. Then a sheepish Franklin arrived with Molly Mandy—dressed, though only just. She was beaming all over her face, and kept on throwing her arms round his neck and kissing him. He smiled quietly. I guess he had finally blown his cherry!

Flowers launched into James Brown and the evening began. I wished I knew where Alex was.

On New Year's Eve it all starts much earlier and by eleven the place was getting pretty jammed. Franco and his boys were doing a great job serving chicken in the basket and champagne—standard fare for the special entrance tickets. Ian Thaine had a table booked for ten, even old Sammy had reserved. The thing was to make it before twelve, and by eleven-thirty a stream of faces appeared. "The Twang," Suki with Massey, three of The Must, a couple of film stars, two members of Parliament, and the whole group of models, photographers and actors who made up the scene.

Then Fontaine looking really fabulous in some kind of fantastic coat. I hoped Franco had somewhere for her to sit as I didn't remember her name being down as having booked. Trust her to try and screw up the table plans.

Why hadn't Alex called me back?

"Funky Broadway" was blasting out, and I laid a smile on my face and went to greet her.

She gave me an ice-cold look and brushed past, followed closely by Ian Thaine, then Vanessa, Leonard and a whole tacky group.

"Hi, Ian," I put out my hand. He squeezed it

limply. "I've been trying to phone you, you're always out."

Vanessa edged forward and I kissed her on the cheek. Her face was flushed and she looked uncomfortable.

Where the hell is Franco? Some schmucky waiter is sitting Fontaine down with Ian.

"Get me Franco, quickly," I hissed to another waiter.

Franco came running over, sweat streaming down his face.

"What's happening here?" I demanded. "Get Mrs. Khaled her own table."

He rushed over to where they were all seated and spoke to Fontaine, then he rushed back to me and said, "Is O.K., Mr. Blake. Mrs. Khaled is with Mr. Thaine's party."

"What?" I couldn't believe my ears. I stared over at the table and caught Fontaine's eye. She smiled coldly at me and then turned to Ian, beside himself with joy.

I had a funny feeling in the pit of my stomach that I had just blown out a deal. Well, screw Ian Thain and his millions. Who needed him anyway? I could find someone else, there must be lots of people who would be only too delighted to put up some loot for me. Yeah, but who?

Some one was throwing paper balls at me. It was the luscious Carla Cassini, squeezed into a black dress with lots of bosom popping out.

" 'Ello, Tonee darling." She purred gaily, sitting safely with her "producer" and several other people. " 'Appy New Year!!" A whole group from Steve Scott's party came rolling in. I was getting loaded. What the hell. Then Sammy with Madelaine—what a daily double! Then Alexandra, I couldn't believe it, my wonderful precious baby had come to see the New Year in with me after all.

I lifted her chin in my hand and smiled softly, "Hello, my lovely." She looked knockout in something pink and soft.

"Hello, Tony—you remember Michael Newcombe don't you?"

Michael the schmuck. What the hell was he doing with her?

"Come on," Maddy shrieked, "let's sit down before midnight. I say, Tony, has Alex told you the super news, she and Michael are engaged! Can you imagine, we're going to be sisters-in-law!"

There comes a time in life when the bottom drops out. When everything just collapses and you don't care about anything. This was it for me. I stared at my Alex in disbelief, and she looked back at me with her big liquid brown eyes, and I felt like I'd been kicked in the stomach by a thousand horses. I made it out to the kitchen and grabbed a bottle of Scotch and drank from it until the fire burned through me.

I've never cried in my life But the kitchen was so goddamned smoky and it gets underneath your eyelids.

Franco came in looking for me.

"Mr. Blake, only five minutes to midnight."

"Yeah, baby." I was out of my skull. I weaved back inside and grabbed the nearest girl.

"Hey," she protested as I dragged her up to the stand next to Flowers.

"O.K. everybody," I yelled. "Make the most of it. Five more glorious minutes—drink up."

The girl pulled herself away from me. "My boy friend will be furious," she said, dashing off.

I got a waiter and told him to get Miss Cassini up here to announce the New Year. Smiling, escorted by two waiters, she was soon beside me, her "producer" beside her.

Flowers was just finishing "Land of a Thousand Dances" and the streamers were flying, balloons popping.

"Here, count down from ten." I handed Carla the mike and she started to count—

"Nine, eight, seven—"

Why had Alex done this to me?

"Six, five, four—"

How *could* she do it?

"Three, two, one—'appy New Year!"

"Auld Lang Syne" blared out and everyone was kissing and laughing and shaking hands. I grabbed Carla and forced my mouth down hard on hers. She struggled and I bit her tongue. Pay the bitch back for that night.

She pushed me away, and her "producer" gave her a stream of abuse in Italian. I laughed and wandered into the crowd. Happy New Year. What was so bleedin' happy about it?

" 'Ere Tony," Sammy was calling me over. "Come and 'ave a drink with us."

"Oh, yes, do," Madelaine urged.

Sure. Sit and watch Alex and Michael gazing into each other's eyes.

"The Twang" appeared and I clung onto her, kissing her fleshy lips and pressing my leg between hers.

"What about you and me later?" I mumbled.

"Oohee, Tony, I can't. I'm with such an important director, and he says there may be a part for me in his next film."

"Yeah, but I've got a part for you now," I leered.

She giggled.

"Come on, come down to the office a minute. I've got something for you."

She hesitated, then thought better of it. "Another night, Tony, I really can't leave this very important director."

Screw her then. The room was spinning. Screw everyone. I could give a good one to Fontaine now. I could really wham it into her the way she liked. I went over to the table. "Happy New Year everyone."

"Thank you, Tony," Fontaine replied, twirling her finger in the champagne glass. "Oh, by the way, masses of luck with your new club. Ian has decided to become partners with me here, so count him out, but lots and lots of luck. I'm sure you'll do very well. Oh, and under the circumstances I think it's best that you don't work here anymore. I've arranged for you to get two weeks' money, so you needn't bother showing up after tonight."

Her face weaved in front of me. Mean cold eyes, thin lips. She ignored me and turned to speak to Ian. They made a good pair. He didn't even dare look anywhere near me. I caught Vanessa peering at me looking concerned, so I laughed. Didn't they all realize that the place would fold without me, anyway?

The noise, the screaming, the bursting of balloons. People tangled up in streamers of colored paper. I want my baby Alex. Where is my darling girl?

I staggered out onto the balcony and shut away the gang bang. The cold air hit me like a punch and my eyes were running. I wished I hadn't drunk so much. I wanted to think clearly, sort things out.

I sat on the ground. It was spitting with rain.

Nice, I'd lost my girl. I'd lost my club. What

was I going to do? I sat there for a bit and then I thought fuck it. So what? There's other girls and there will be other clubs. Life is *great* baby. So I went back inside and drank and danced and shouted and burst balloons and threw streamers, and drank drank drank.

Then Hal appeared with his old dreamboat Mamie.

"Hey, Tony sweetheart, Mamie and I got married, say congratulations."

I looked at Hal. The last of the great promoters was finally caught. Mamie was smiling and clinging fondly to his arm. She could have been his mother.

"We flew in from Rome to sign some papers. I'm taking over the studio, you know."

What studio? "Great!" I tried to smile.

Mamie beamed. "Tony dear, this is my very dear friend Delphine Cohen from Miami. This is her first trip to Europe and Hally and I are going to show her the sights."

Delphine Cohen was dyed blond somewhere in her late fifties. I nodded at her. She showed me a lot of teeth.

We all sat down and I ordered champagne. Sammy came hopping over to see what was up. Mamie and Delphine went off to the ladies' room and Hal immediately grabbed a hold of me.

"Listen, Tony, don't be a schmuck! I know

it's not your scene but Delphine Cohen's old man practically *owned* Miami, and he dropped off with a heart attack six months ago, so she's hot as a pistol raring to go. What are you going to do, hang around this joint all your life? Smarten up fellow, look at me. I'm a big man now."

I looked at Hal. He was so stoned his eyes held a permanent glaze.

Mamie and Delphine came back and we drank more champagne. Franco kept rushing over to me with minor dramas, but I told him to stuff 'em. Hobo wasn't my bag any more. Let someone else run his ass off.

Delphine had plump arms with freckles. I suppose she wasn't too bad for an older bird. Oh, boy, more champagne. Much, much more.

Mamie was saying, "Tony why don't you come to Rome with us for a few days? Hally's so busy now and we need a man to protect us on the streets. It's true what they say about the Italian men, poor Delphine's black and blue!"

Poor Delphine laughed and jangled a heavy diamond bracelet in time to the music. I wondered if I could make it? I wondered if I *should* make it?

Hal gave me a wink. "Yeah, come to Rome, baby, we'll have a great time. What do you say, Delphine?"

"Sure," she smiled at me, "wonderful idea.

Will you come?" Her eyes lingered on my face, asking their own personal question.

I stood up abruptly. "Yeah, maybe. I'll have to see. Excuse me, got to see what's going on. I'll be back in a minute." I rushed out to the desk.

"Happy New Year, Mr. Blake," said Tina.

A group of people were coming in, girls dressed up like Christmas trees. Automatically I went into the whole greeting bit. One of the girls was fantastic, long dark hair with pearls, a white-fringed trouser outfit, staring green eyes. Someone introduced us, her name was Miranda.

She smiled at me and licked full pink lips.

I felt a familiar stirring, which I knew I should be keeping for Delphine Cohen. I grabbed her by the arm and took her off to dance.

Flowers was freaking out on Clarence Carter. I gave him the signal and he switched to Jose Feliciano's "Light My Fire."

Miranda was tall and soft in my arms. I held onto her tightly. To hell with Delphine Cohen and all her loot. I wasn't getting caught in one of those sick scenes again.

So I'll be busted out. So what? Something will come along, something that I won't have to sell myself for. And if it doesn't? Well that's life. I can always wash dishes.

The girl in my arms isn't Alex, but she is certainly a beautiful girl. Creamy skin, and bright eyes.

"I wasn't expecting to meet anyone like you tonight," I whispered, pulling her a little closer.

"Me neither," she said, laughing softly. "I only flew in from New York yesterday. I thought Englishmen had a reputation for being all uptight and stuffy."

"What do you think now?"

She just pushed her body hard against mine.

We danced and danced. Hal and his group eventually left. "Schmuck!" he came up and muttered to me. "You're blowing a great setup for another ding-a-ling."

Fontaine swept out after three with her entourage, Ian Thaine smirking at her heels.

I didn't see my Alex go, I didn't want to. I just wanted to forget her.

Miranda and I left at six in the morning. She was trailing a load of balloons and we walked through the deserted streets to my pad.

I loved her face. It was serious and sexy. She had a boy's firm body with lovely small breasts, and I had to push her long dark hair away to kiss them.

"I just got disengaged when I left," she said as I explored her with my hands. "My fiancé could only make it in group scenes. Ugh! I hated that. My daddy said I should fly off somewhere and forget about him. He certainly knew what he was talking about. Oh, I love *that!*"

"My fiancé just got engaged to someone else."

"How awful. Oh, oh, oh—do *that* again! You should come to New York to forget."

"Yeah." I climbed on top of her. She was a gorgeous girl. "With what?"

She wriggled around. "Hey, Tony, you're fantastic! Just too much! Listen. I know. You can come and work for my daddy, he's got all sorts of businesses. Oh—wow! Happy New Year! Baby, baby, baby! Do that again. We've got this disco in New York called Pickett's. It would be just right for you and, ooh, Tony, that's so beautiful, so wild. I love it! Like yes! Wowee Tony—you're such a stud!"